# Where Ashes Flow

## TOM AVILA

ISBN-10: 1499378025
ISBN-13: 9781499378023

# DEDICATION

To my loving wife and inspiration

# CONTENTS

# ACKNOWLEDGMENTS

This being my first book, I reached out for help in many different directions. I'd like to thank those who were kind enough to give of their time and valued expertise.

Linda Chase: She helped me take my first baby steps as a writer.

Darv Averill: My old cowboy buddy who introduced me to the rodeo world, wild Cowboy bars and over the years, all the fantastic trips into the beautiful Bob Marshall Wilderness. I believe Darv is the best fly fisherman I've ever seen.

Fran Simmons: Thank you for all your cheers and support and your dedicated adoration for my story. Fran made sure every T was crossed and every I was dotted.

Robert Avila: My brother. The brains of the family, I always said. He is a brilliant editor who guided me through many pit falls and steered me always in the right direction.

Danielle: My oldest daughter. Thanks, for the perfect cover design, I love it.

Linda: What can I say? Without her there would be no story. She's my beautiful wife, the mother of our children and she gave me the most amazing and wonderful life. She was a severe critic and would often say after reading a page, "No, you're being lazy." then send me off to rewrite. She also gave me constant encouragement and unending love...

# PROLOGUE

The sky exploded in a slashing streak of brilliant light and the rumbling sound of thunder echoed off the canyon walls as the ground trembled, causing ripples on the river below. The rain continued sporadically but by morning, the night's storm was gone. You could still see its remnants on the drying granite in black streaks of moisture in the canyon walls and hear it in the sound of the river rushing over the rocks on its way down into the valley.

A hundred feet above the river, on the canyon wall, a narrow, rocky trail cut its way across the face of the canyon and then faded into the trees on the other side. Two riders suddenly appeared through the thick forest at one edge of the canyon and stopped their horses for a moment. Then they slowly rode across the face of the steep cliff. From their vantage point, the canyon wall dropped straight down into the raging river. When they reached the other side, they vanished into the trees, and began working their way down a narrow trail that wound its way through tall pines and aspen before reaching the rocky bank of the river.

The man and his daughter rode up to the rushing water and dismounted to let their horses rest.

"Dad, are you crazy?" The young girl leaned across her horse toward her father so he could see the fear on her face.

"Crazy. What are you talking about?"

"Come on Dad; that stupid trail on the side of the cliff."

"Yeah, that's some view from up there."

"I'm not talking about the view."

"Were you scared?"

"Well, yeah, we could have been killed."

"Don't get all excited. I'll take you back another way, okay?"

"There's another way? But you took me across that scary cliff instead?"

"Now, relax. I thought you might enjoy the view."

"What view? I was so scared, I was afraid to look."

"There's nothing to worry about. That's a good, safe trail and the horses know what they're doing. I'd never put you in harm's way. You know that. You're just not used to riding on mountain trails."

It was the early fifties and the country was changing, changing too fast for her father. But today, he was spending a rare, wonderful afternoon with his young daughter, and he was going to enjoy it. He was 48, a strong good-looking man, average in height, with a full head of grey hair. It was late August, and his lovely daughter Emma, her stark white skin now tanned from the summer sun, was just turning 15. Her days spent in the sun had brought out little brown freckles; now sprinkled across her cheeks and nose. She hated her freckles and often tried to conceal them with makeup. When she laughed, her bright blue eyes sparkled, and when her auburn hair moved in the breeze, it let the sun light shine through with golden highlights. She was so pretty, people often stopped and stared. Emma had a fear of heights, but she always kept it to herself. If her father had known this, he never would have taken her across the face of the cliff. He felt overwhelming love for his daughter, his only child, and knew without hesitation that he'd give his life if needed to protect her from danger.

Emma had a natural-born instinct for riding horses, and being young and competitive, she loved to show it off with her friends in barrel racing and other timing events. She loved the speed and excitement. There was something magical about sitting on a live, hot-blooded animal, running him at top speed with the wind in your face and the sound of hoofs pounding in the ground. This was the free spirit she drew from this most beautiful animal. There were occasions when she rode her horse in the local parade and the grand entry, when the rodeo came to town. But now she was in unfamiliar territory. This was her first trip into the high mountains, a new and somewhat frightening experience. She was not racing her horse around obstacle in an arena but walking up and down narrow cliffs where the shale would sometimes break loose from under the horse's hoofs and slide down the hill-side.

Her father walked along the river, looking for the easiest place to cross. He didn't want to scare his daughter any more than he already had. "We can cross here." He pointed to the bank where the river was at its narrowest point. "The river is low this time of year so we shouldn't have any problems." Walking over to his daughter, he put his arm around her shoulder and smiled. "We might get our feet wet, but that's about it."

She looked up at his proud, smiling face, "Don't worry, Dad, I'll be fine now. It's the heights that I don't like." They mounted their horses and started towards the water, and then he stopped and turned. "Look over there." He motioned with a nod of his head. "See that emerald green water where the river flows around the cliff? You can tell it's really deep, because of the color. You get your horse in there; you'd be in a mess of trouble." He said, relishing in the moment, "Are you ready to get your feet wet?"

"Anytime you are."

"The footing's rocky, with some good-size boulders, so be careful. Your horse might stumble, but don't worry, he'll be fine."

After crossing the river, the trail turned back up into the mountains. They traversed through the trees on what now was a rough poorly groomed trail. At times they lost sight of it completely in the overgrown brush and broken branches. But the horses kept up a steady pace, showing no signs of strain or fatigue.

"Look, Dad, up there. A tree has fallen across the trail. What are we going to do?" She asked hoping they would just turn around and head back.

"We're fine. We'll just ride up and go around it."

"But Dad, it's so steep, can the horses make it?"

"They'll make it. Just give your horse a good kick." Emma sat on her horse and watched her father as he turned his horse into the hillside and put his spurs into the horse's flank. It leaped up the hill and pulled itself around the tree and back down to the trail on the other side. "That's a good boy." He patted his horse on the neck. "Ok, baby, that's all you have to do. He'll just follow what my horse did."

Emma looked over the top of the large tree trunk at her father waiting on the other side, an apprehensive smile on her face. "You made it look so easy."

"It was. Come on, you can do it." Emma turned her horse to the hillside, leaned forward, and gave him her best kick, and up they went around the tree to her father's side.

"Now that wasn't too bad, was it?" He leaned over to her, offering a handshake.

"How much farther is it?" was her only response to his friendly query.

He looked up and motioned with his hand to the top of the hill. "See that large boulder up there? Well, it's right on the other side. Do you think you can make it that much farther?"

He was seeing her start to lose interest in their trail ride. Emma was very young and probably had a thousand other things on her mind, and riding to the top of a mountain with her father on a warm summer day most likely wasn't one of them.

"Sure. No problem."

"Once we get past that large boulder up there, it will start to flatten out into the prettiest little meadow."

As they rode past it, she was finally able to take a deep breath and relax. She stopped her horse and gazed at her surroundings. Its beauty and the spectacular setting overwhelmed her. Lush green grass grew everywhere, and the meadow was surrounded by a thick grove of Aspen trees, just now starting to turn colors. Right in the center of the meadow was a small lake that looked like a mirror reflecting the bright blue sky and the grass along its banks. It was beyond the imagination. Everything appeared so green for this time of year. Emma began to listen to the sounds around her. "I can hear water, but where is it coming from?"

"From over there." He pointed to the far edge of the meadow, "This is where the creek that runs by our cabin starts. It boils out of the ground from an underground river and creates Bear Creek, which runs down into the river valley, and eventually it all ends up in the ocean."

"Gee, that's really neat. It's so pretty I've never seen anything like it. That little lake over there, it doesn't look real. It looks like no one's ever been here before."

"I don't think many people know about this place, and if they do, they never seem to come up here."

"I can sure understand that, after that hairy ride."

"This was your mother's and my favorite place. We used to ride up here on hot summer days and go skinny-dipping in that lake," he said, drifting off into distant memories. "She used to joke that you were conceived up here."

"Ok, Dad, I really don't need to hear that kind of information. I'm your daughter, not one of your guy friends." She turned and slapped him on his arm.

"I'm sorry... but it's true."

They spent some time riding their horses around as her father showed her the area. They talked and laughed and enjoyed the afternoon together. They seldom had time to be alone with each other. So today was turning out to be a special day for both of them.

Her father stopped his horse and got off. "Get down. We'll let the horses graze for a while." He put his arm around her shoulder. "Come with me, I want to show you something."

They walked over where the water was bubbling out of the earth. "Be careful on the rocks, they're slippery," He took a deep breath and looked down at the water rising up from under the ground. "This is why I brought you up here."

"Is there a special reason?"

He saw the confused expression on her face.

"Yes, for me it's very special." He held her hand and began to explain. "My father, your grandfather, was in the Navy during World War I. The Germans attacked his ship. They managed to fight them off, but my father was killed in the battle. He was buried at sea. They laid him on a board, covered him with a flag, and slid him into the cold, black ocean. I want to have a say in where I end up. I don't want to be just dumped somewhere. I want to go from start to finish. I want to go from the stream to the creek, to the river to the ocean. I want to cover the whole gamut. When I die, I want you to have me cremated and bring my ashes here."

"Dad, don't talk like that. You're not going to die."

"Well of course I'm going to die; we're all going to die someday."

"I know, Dad, but this is so morbid."

"This isn't morbid. The mountains, streams, rivers, and valleys, even the ocean, are all things I have loved about living. That's why I want you to do this for me. I want you to drop my ashes in at this spot right here. So they'll go all the way down Bear Creek, past our cabin, and down to the river and into the ocean. Can you do that for me?"

"Well, yeah, I guess so. It all sounds a little silly."

"It won't seem silly when the time comes."

"I might do it, if I can find an easier way up here."

"Hopefully by then you'll be a lot older, and the ride won't seem difficult to you."

They walked around and talked awhile longer, just watching the scenery and the horses grazing. "This is such a quiet and peaceful place," he said. "It's perfect."

Emma walked up to her dad and put her arms around him and held him tight. She wanted him to know how much he meant to her and how much she loved him. "Yes Dad, this is the perfect place."

He looked down at her and smiled, "We should probably start back. Your mother is going to be worried. It will be dark by the time we get to the cabin."

"Alright, but I hope you know a better way back."

He grinned as they mounted their horses. "I'll take you back the easy way. It's a little longer, but there're no steep cliffs. Okay?"

"Okay."

The cabin was about six miles away and, yes, there was an easier way back. She knew that he just wanted to show off for her and give her a good scare for her money. She had been scared all right, up on that cliff, but all in all it was a fabulous day, one she would never trade away nor ever forget. He told her not to mention the bit about the ashes to her mother. She would just get upset.

Emma never forgot that trip. At the time she didn't think much about it, but as years went by and she grew into an adult, she began to realize how meaningful it was, but she never could have imagined what affect it would have on their lives. She talked about it often and about the ashes, never knowing what lay ahead for them.

# CHAPTER ONE

The past kept haunting the old cowboy as he sat on his horse on a broken ridgeline that looked out over the small town he now called home. He recalled this story Emma, his wife, had told him many times about her father and their trek into the mountains when she was only fifteen and the promise she made to him that day.

He moved his horse up the ridge to the flats where the short, sparse grass blew lightly in the breeze and dismounted. He let the rains fall to the ground, and his horse stood and didn't move. He turned his back, leaned against his horse and looked out to the east where the sun was slowly rising behind the low clouds above the horizon. He took his hat off and hung it on the horn of the saddle, then turned, unbuckled his saddlebags and lifted out a .38 Colt revolver.

He sat down on the cold ground, stretching his legs out straight, and turned the gun over in his hands, then halfcocked the hammer and spun the cylinder and pressed its cold steel against his heart. He sat there for a long time, holding the gun firm in his hands and staring off into the distance.

His horse suddenly backed off a step and raised its head, its ears alert. He turned to follow the horse's movement and saw three riders cresting the hill a half-mile away to the west. He got to his feet and let the hammer back down and put the gun back in the saddlebag, took up the reins, mounted his horse and started down the hillside, his thoughts once again drifting back in time.

The day began to warm as he walked his horse along the ridge that over looked homes and the small town. A tall, slender man in his mid-seventies, the old cowboy sat loose in the saddle as he looked back over his shoulder. The three riders were far away now, on the other side of the hill. He stopped his horse and wiped tears away with his shirtsleeve, tears that seemed to come out of nowhere. His wide-brim hat cast a shadow over his red-rimmed eyes, and the lines in his unshaven face seem deeper and more pronounced than ever. Just like the jeans he wore, the threads of his life were frayed and faded.  On the back of his old leather belt, his name, Q U I N N, could be read in tarnished silver letters, his trophy buckle for calf roping, dated 1957.  A lot had happened in the past forty-five years. To him, it all seemed like yesterday, and now all the yesterdays were slipping away.

He turned his horse around and started back down the hill towards the homes below.  At the bottom of the hill, he rode along an embankment above a small creek, passed under a large Sycamore then down into the creek bed as a flock of crows scattered from the trees, squawking and circling overhead.  When he reached the water, he stopped his horse to drink.  He took off his hat and held it up to shade his eyes, observing the birds gliding freely around in the sky, then looked back at the water as the sun's reflection flickered in his eyes: This small creek could be a rushing river during heavy rain storms, but today it was just slow-moving water with no sense of urgency or direction, except downhill.

He pushed his hair back with his hand and slid his hat back on, then crossed the creek and climbed up the bank on the other side, like they'd done so many times before.  He took this ride almost every day now.  Things seemed clearer to him, on his rides.  It was the only time when the grief didn't hurt his soul.  These were the times when he could remember and think, and sometimes even try to forget.

His wife Emma had been gone almost a year now.  Has it been almost a year?  He thought, has it really been that long? Emma's death was not completely unexpected.  She had been sick and fighting cancer off and on for years.  But the shock of her loss was not easy for him.  It hit hard, harder than expected.  He'd known it was coming and he thought he was ready for it, he thought he could handle it.  He had just lost his partner in life, his lover and best friend; all at once everything was gone.  They'd been together for almost a half-century; her death left a deep void in his world.

He rode up another small hill that led to a bridle path, then rode along behind some homes and down to a street; crossed the street and picked up the trail again.  He continued on towards a large grassy park; on weekends it's full of children playing soccer, but today it's quiet, the way he liked it.

It was almost eleven o'clock by the time he started up the narrow street, towards his house.  Tall trees shaded this quiet neighborhood of small single-story homes, built sometime during the early sixties. They were all one acre lots, and most of the residents stabled horses.

He rode up the driveway and around to the back of the house to a small barn and corral, dismounted and stood motionless for a few moments. His legs felt stiff and he stretched them out before moving about. He put his arm around his horse's neck and slipped the halter on and removed the saddle. His eyes now obscured with mist; he began to brush the warm sweaty back of his horse. He looked down and seemed lost in thought as the brushing continued; over and over, repeating the same stroke, again and again, until finally his horse turned its head and looked back as if anxious for the brushing to end. The old cowboy's head snapped up and he gave one final stroke of the brush before leading him into the stall. He shut the stall door and watched as his horse wandered out into the corral then he turned and slowly walked to the house.

Emma's little white dog Sugar was turning in circles, waiting for him as he opened the door, and before he knew it she had jumped into his arms and began licking his face. He walked her over to the lawn in the backyard and set her down on the grass. He'd been riding up in the hills all morning and knew she was ready for a pee break. After Sugar finished her deed, she immediately followed him back into the house, constantly trying to keep his attention.

He walked over to the coffee pot, poured himself a cup of cold coffee left over from earlier that morning and stuck it in the microwave. When it was heated, he took it out and sat down at the kitchen table. Sipping his coffee, he gazed upon a shiny gold box sitting on the table in front of him. He sat there for a long time staring at it, until his coffee got cold again. He reheated it and walked through the kitchen into the den. The den was in the back of the house, with a large window that looked out towards the barn and corral. He could see his reflection in the window, and through his reflection he saw his horse in the corral, staring back and the sadness returned. Then he listened and thought he heard Emma's voice, as clearly as if she were standing next to him and he drifted back in time. "Honey, you're going to be sixty-seven this year. I would sure like to see you on a better mount."

"You never did like that mare, did you?"

"No, I think she's crazy and could hurt you some day."

"There isn't a mean bone in her body. But I must admit, I've thought about looking around for a good mountain horse."

Emma knew her condition was not improving—she just wasn't getting better, and it was only a matter of time. But there were things she had to take care of first. If something were to happen to her husband, she couldn't take care of him, and besides, she was going to need him in the months to come. She knew how he loved to ride. He had been riding horses his entire life, it was his only outlet. Riding had become his escape from what was really going on in their life.

He never thought about getting hurt, but Emma was right, he wasn't getting any younger. He had slowed down some in the past few years and he knew it. His body wasn't reacting as quickly as it once did. Maybe she was right, she usually was. Emma had a special gift of knowing things before they happened. You could call it intuition. But whatever it was, she was good at it, and when she had these moments, she just knew she was right.

Emma turned to him and smiled. "Well, I'm glad you feel that way, because your brother called from the ranch while you were out riding. Will said he had four new horses he just got in from Texas. He mentioned one big bay gelding that he thought you might be interested in."

"Oh, I see, you've already started the ball rolling."

"Sometimes you need a little nudge to get started," she chuckled.

"A nudge, it feels more like a shove."

"I told him you would drive over and try him out this afternoon."

"This afternoon? He wants me out there today?"

"Do you have other plans?"

"No, it just seems sudden, that's all."

"I think you should go. Besides, he's expecting you."

"Well. I guess there's no reason why I can't. Do you feel up to going? I'd like to see what you think, before I make an investment."

"No, you go ahead. I'm a little tired today, and you know what will work for you. When you get back, you can tell me all about it."

Emma and Quinn had sold their interest in the ranch to Quinn's brother Will and his wife Barbara. They had three boys, and they all wanted to be involved in ranching. Emma and Quinn's girls, Anna and Jessica, were both married and had moved away. They had started their own families, and neither of them was interested in ranching. When Emma first got sick, they purchased the house on an acre of land near town and moved in. It was close to doctors and the new hospital that was being built. Quinn still went to the ranch and helped out when needed. But a great deal of his time was spent helping Emma and taking her to her treatments.

Will was standing in the corral when Quinn arrived at the ranch. The horse was already saddled and ready to ride.

"Boy, you sure don't waste any time when it comes to moving a horse, do you?" Quinn remarked, leaning out the window of his truck.

"This one is going fast." Will replied, "Get out and come over and take a good look."

Quinn opened the door and stepped out. He stood looking over the corral fence at his brother and the fine-looking animal standing next to him.

"The ranch looks great. You must be working the boys' tails off."

"Trying to keep them busy and out of trouble."

"I always thought getting into trouble was your job."

"Not anymore. They're much better at it than I ever was."

Quinn laughed. "I doubt that. No one knew trouble like you did."

"Those days are long gone."

Quinn had a hard time taking his eyes off the horse as he stepped through the fence rails into the corral. He could tell there was something special about him. "I want to thank you for calling Emma. She's been trying to keep me out of harm's way now that I'm getting up there in age. Realizing the fact that you're an old man isn't easy."

"I know what you mean, I'm right behind you." Will looked at the horse and turned towards Quinn "When I first saw him, I thought of you. He kind of reminds me of that old mountain horse that Mom had. Do you remember?"

"Yeah, you're right, they do look a lot alike. How could I ever forget that horse? He was really a fine animal and could cover a lot of ground."

Quinn walked over and put his hand out and rubbed the horse's nose. The four-year-old bay gelding was a beautiful quarter horse, fifteen three hands high. He was reddish brown with a black mane and tail, two white socks on his hind legs and a white star on his forehead. He stood straight and quiet.

"Go ahead and take him for a spin."

"He sure is a pretty boy. What's his name?"

"He doesn't have a name. I'll leave that up to the new owner."

Quinn took the reins from his brother and mounted. The horse remained still and waited for a command. Quinn could tell instantly what he had under the saddle. The response of this horse was amazing. Quinn walked him around the arena and then put him in a slow lope. He stopped, spun the horse to the right, stopped, spun him to the left, then loped him to the end of the arena, stopped, rolled him back, and loped him over to where Will was standing.

"He sure is responsive." Quinn said. "I wonder why they gelded him. I bet he would have made a great stud."

"I wondered the same thing, but he would've cost me more."

"Well... whoever cut this horse should have his lopped off. Open the gate for me, Will. I want to take him up into the hills. Okay                            with                            you?"

"Sure, take him anywhere you want." Quinn started off for the hill. Will stood holding the open gate, watching him until he was out of sight. Quinn was gone about forty-five minutes, and as he rode back, he couldn't wipe the grin off his face.

"Looks like someone had a good time." Will knew Quinn and knew what he liked in a horse. This was a once-in-a-lifetime find, and there was no way Quinn could pass on it.

"Boy, he's sure a sweetheart of a horse." Quinn felt it in his gut; he knew this horse was special. "You must have spent a bundle for him. He's got to be way out of my bracket. Do you have a long-term payment plan for horses like this?"

"Not for this horse. I've already sold him."

"You've sold him!? Then why the hell did you put me through this?"

"Because Emma bought him for you yesterday, and he's paid in full. He's in your bracket now. Say, Bracket sounds like a good name for a horse. I like it. Bracket. What do you think, Quinn?"

Quinn shook his head in disbelief. "That little rascal; she never said a thing to me."

12

"Well, it's true. He's all yours. Have you ever ridden a better horse?"

"No, I sure haven't."

"You have a good woman there, Quinn. You take good care of her."

Quinn was still in shock over the entire transaction. He answered his brother in a soft, low voice. "Yeah, I'll take good care of her, but I can't believe she did this."

"Oh, by the way, she said to tell you happy Father's Day."

The little white dog started barking and jumping up on Quinn's legs, snapping him back to reality. He blinked and looked around the room. Sugar was sitting at his feet, wagging her tail. He wiped his eyes with his fingers and said to Sugar, "Come with me," and turned around and walked to the bedroom and stretched out on his bed. Sugar jumped up and lay next to him and he stroked her lightly and shut his eyes and told his brain to slow down and let him be. Death is so permanent; you don't get a trial run to see how you'd handle it. Once it comes, it's there forever.

What do you do with a whole day? Quinn just wandered from room to room, chair to chair, sofa to outside and back in again, not knowing how to speed up the days. After a morning ride, he'd come home and spend the rest of the day waiting for it to end. Was this living, or just another form of death?

Quinn couldn't understand how he lost control; he'd always been the strong one, the one who took care of her. He'd hold her and watched over her. He was the one who never broke, the one who took charge. "What happened to me?" he wondered. I can't even take care of myself.

## CHAPTER TWO

The wind and rain never let up all night. Images of Emma; mixed up with the storm, just added to Quinn's insomnia. He tossed and turned in his bed, trying to find that one position that would let his body rest. But the sleep he so desperately wanted was not to be. Sleep was the one thing that protected him. It's a sad existence when you wake-up in the morning looking forward to the evening so you can go to sleep.

Some nights when he dosed off, he'd awaken in a cold sweat, by what sounded like a voice whispering words he couldn't understand. He'd sit up in bed and glance around, as if there were someone in the room, then get out of bed and walk to the window and stared out into the darkness, until the chill of the night air sent him back to his bed and finally to sleep only to wake up in the morning exhausted. This was occurring more and more frequently, and he was beginning to worry about his state of mind.

It was early spring, and the days were starting to get longer. In the morning when Quinn walked into the kitchen; the sun streaming through the window cast rays of sunlight across the room and onto the table where the gold box sat. Each morning, as the days grew longer, the sun's rays moved closer and closer to the gold box.

One morning as he walked in, a flicker of light startled him. He held his hand up to shield his eyes and looked over and saw the sunlight reflecting off the gold box. He moved slowly over towards the table, his body blocking the sun. He stood there, looking down at the box. "What are you trying to tell me?" he said, reaching out with his hand, his fingers gently touching the top. It was the first time he had touched it since he had picked it up from the mortuary months ago and placed it there on the table. "What is it Emma, what do you want me to do?" He sat down in a chair at the table and took the box in his hands and held it tight. He felt an overwhelming sadness. "I know you. You're trying to tell me something. God knows, I can almost hear you."

Quinn got up from the table, walked over, picked up the phone and called his daughter.

"Anna, its Dad."

"I've been worried about you, Dad. Is everything alright?"

"Yeah, everything's fine. I haven't felt much like talking."

"Well, I get worried when I don't hear from you."

"I know. I'm sorry. We probably should talk more."

"It's real hard on me, too, Dad." Quinn could tell that Anna had started to cry. "I'm sorry, just a minute, Dad." He could hear Anna scolding her daughter in the background. "Eva-Marie, go get ready for school. I don't want you to be late again this morning."

"Is everything alright honey?"

"Yeah, I'm sorry." She hesitated, her voice sounding sad. "You know it wasn't Eva-Marie's fault that she was late… It was my fault. Some mornings I just can't seem to get myself together. Sometimes when the phone rings… I think its Mother calling. I've even caught myself picking up the phone to call her… then realizing she's gone. I miss those mornings… we could talk for hours." Her voice began to tremble. "I miss her so much every day… You're my dad and I need to talk to you sometimes. You know what I mean, Dad?"

"I know, honey. I feel the same way."

"You do, Dad?"

"Yes, I just wander around from room to room waiting for the days to pass."

"It's hard, isn't it?"

"Yes it is. But I promise you, it will get better."

"I hope you're right."

"I know I'm right." He said it to her, but in his heart he didn't think things would ever get better. "Say, look, I thought I might go up and open the cabin. It's that time of year, and I think the trip will be good for me. What do you think?"

Anna's voice was now in control and sounded concerned. "I don't know, Dad. I don't think that's a good idea, not by yourself anyway."

"I'll be fine. I've done it a hundred times."

There was a pause. He could hear muffled voices as if she had her hand over the receiver and was talking to someone. Quinn knew that Robert and Anna, as kids will do, were having words about the old man. Then she came back on the phone.

16

"Robert was just leaving for work. He said if you'll wait 'til the end of the month, he'll go up with you. You shouldn't drive up alone"

"It's not just about opening the cabin…It's something I have to do…by myself. I can't explain it. You're going to have to trust me, Anna. I want to be alone."

"I know how you feel Dad, but I don't like to see you driving all that way by yourself."

"I've made that drive so many times I could do it with my eyes closed."

There was a long pause. "Well… I can't stop you… but if anything should happen to you…"

He cut her off, "Nothing is going to happen! I'll call you and check in, okay?"

"Alright, but you better call."

"I will, I promise. I'm going to leave Sugar. Could you take care of her till I get back? I don't think I'll be gone that long."

"Sure. I'll come by and pick her up tomorrow."

"Thanks, I really appreciate it. I'm going to take Bracket with me so you don't have to worry about him."

"I love you Dad and you be careful and call, you hear me?"

"I love you too honey."

When he hung up the phone, he went back and sat down again at the table. That was probably the longest conversation he'd had in over three months. He just didn't like to talk much. His voice felt weak, and the emotions of the short conversation seemed to have drained him. His daughter Anna had become the backbone of the family. She was now the one who planned all the holiday events. She was the one determined not to let the family splinter apart. She was a pretty girl in her late thirties. Like her mother Emma, she could also turn heads with her good looks. Anna was blond with blue eyes and olive skin like her fathers. She got pregnant her junior year of college, married her college sweetheart and started having children. Her husband Robert was a tall nice looking man with premature graying hair. He went into the insurance business with his father. They lived just on the other side of town. Just far enough away that it wasn't convenient to drop by daily to see each other.

After the phone call, Quinn sat at the table with the box in front of him. It felt warm as he held it in his hands. He slowly removed the top. He set the top on the table and looked inside.

17

There was a plastic bag full of her ashes, fastened securely at the top. Quinn pulled the bag out of the box and set it on the table. He stared at it, and his body shivered. He couldn't get over the fact that they were his wife's ashes. How could you put all those years of love and companionship into a small plastic bag? Oh my God, he realized, this is all there is left. He picked the bag up and held it out in front of him with both hands as if he was offering it to someone. The box was warm, but the bag with the ashes felt cold. He pressed the bag to his lips and set it back down, then quickly pushed himself away from the table, stood up and moved over to the sink. He turned the cold water on and splashed his face. "I don't know if I can do this," he muttered.

Quinn was in bed by 9:30 that evening, hoping he'd get a good night's sleep and leave for the cabin before the sunrise. He knew the weather was unpredictable at that time of year, so he wanted to get an early start. His mind kept spinning as he lay still and tried to quiet his thoughts, so he'd sleep. But the sleep never came. He was still wide awake at eleven o'clock. He threw the covers back, got up and dressed. Sugar sat on the bed and watched, wondering what happened to their night of sleep.

Quinn stepped outside onto the porch and looked around, trying to remember all the things he had to do. He knew he should write things down, but he never seemed to have pen or pencil handy or even something to write on. So he just listed everything in his head, but that hasn't been working well as of late. He stood there thinking, rubbing the whiskers on his chin, looked up into the sky and took a deep breath. The air felt cool and fresh after the light rain that evening. He put his hat on and walked down the steps and across the yard into the barn, where he took his saddlebags down off a shelf. He grabbed an old towel that was hanging on a hook and wiped the dust from the bags, then carried them back to the house. He set the saddlebags on the table, opened up one side and carefully placed the bag that held his wife's ashes inside and buckled them in tight. He thought it might be sacrilegious, putting her ashes in an old leather saddlebag like that, but he wanted them close by his side when he rode up to the mountain. What safer place could there be then to have her there, right next to him? It seemed no matter what Quinn was doing, he kept feeling this weight of grief pressing down on him, and he was hoping the drive to the cabin would lighten the pressure.

This time as he stepped out of the house, he felt a slight mist in the air but still no sign of any rain. He reached into his pocket for his keys as he walked over to his pickup, opened the door and placed the saddlebags behind the front seat and slid in on the cold seat, turned the key in the ignition, started the truck and backed it to the trailer; then hitched it up. He pulled the truck and trailer forward to the open covered shed where he kept his hay and labored up a three-string bail of Timothy hay onto the bed of his pickup. He pushed the bale up close to the cab, covered it with a black tarp and secured it with bungee cords. He climbed down, went into the barn, found a small canvas bag with drawstrings and filled it with crimped oats and a scoop of soybean meal. He put the bag behind the front seat, next to the saddlebags, drove the truck and trailer to the front driveway, parked and got out. He walked around behind the trailer and checked the tail lights. Satisfied that the lights were working he went back to the house. Inside he gathered up a bag with his clothes and a box full of things he'd need when he got to the cabin.

Sugar kept running around and standing on her hind legs looking up at him. Once she had even jumped into his bag before he zipped it up. She kept looking up at him, starring with those big dark eyes. Sugar was begging to come along. "You're going to stay here," he told her. "I can't take you" When Quinn went back outside, Sugar ran to the window and watched with anticipation as he loaded the truck.

He walked out to the corral, put a halter on Bracket, led him to the trailer and loaded him in. He opened the tack room door of the trailer and put his saddle and the rest of his tack inside. Then got back in his truck and sat thinking about what he might have forgotten. He wanted to make sure he wasn't leaving anything behind. His mind was spinning. He had to slow down and think. What was he missing? Quinn opened the door, stepped out and reached behind the seat for his saddlebags. He opened up both sides and it wasn't there. What did he do with it? It was gone. He walked back into the barn. From a shelf above the workbench he pulled down a wooden box and set it on the bench. He opened it, and inside was his father's pearl handle .38-caliber Colt revolver and a box of shells. He must have put it back and not remembered. He took the gun out of the box and held it in the light.

The gun was shiny and felt slick in his hands. He was just a young man the last time he had fired this gun, fifty years ago. He couldn't remember why he'd shot the gun or at what. You'd think something like that would stay clear in his mind forever. He'd been trying hard to hold on to his memories but that one was gone now. He wanted to take it with him if he needed a way out. Time has a way of healing bad wounds. Sometimes it's not worth waiting, when there's no reason to be here any longer. She's gone and he was alone now, so what's left. Was he just feeling sorry for himself, or what? He still had family, then why did he feel so lost and alone?

Quinn passed the gun back and forth from hand to hand. He then opened the cylinder and put six bullets in it and walked back to the truck. He put the gun in the saddlebag next to Emma's ashes. As he started the truck and pulled forward past the kitchen door, he could see Sugar looking at him through the window. She started barking and jumping as he drove by her, down to the end of the driveway.

Sugar was full of excitement as the window in front of her turned bright red from the reflection from the brake lights, and she became awash in a reddish tint. A moment later Quinn came sauntering back, opened the door and picked her up. He wrote a short note to Anna. I decided to take Sugar with me. Thanks anyway, love Dad.

Quinn opened the truck door and put Sugar on the seat next to him. He slid in beside her and scratched her behind the ear. "So you want to go for a ride, do you? Well, make yourself comfortable, we have a long ways to go." Again he started up the truck and finally took off. They drove up the small tree-lined street to the corner and turned left toward the highway that would take them to the interstate.

There was a gas station just before the on ramp to the interstate. Quinn pulled in next to a gas pump, filled the truck with gas and checked the oil. He walked inside to get a cup of coffee, picked up some dog food and went to pay his bill. Behind the counter he noticed a rack of cigars. "I'll take two of those sweet Palmita cigars." He motioned with his hand to the attendant. "Ok, anything else?"

"No, I guess that's it. You know, the last time I smoked one of these expensive cigars was at my daughter's wedding. That was nine years ago."

"Well, I hope you enjoy these just as much." The attendant replied with a courteous smile. Quinn finished paying his bill and went back to the truck.

"That's it, Sugar, we're on our way. No more stops." He picked up the interstate and headed towards the mountains.

As he merged onto the rain-slick highway he began to recall the afternoon three years earlier when the nightmare began. It started out innocent enough on a warm Sunday in early August. He and Emma were expecting Quinn's old rodeo buddy, Deek Keller, and his new bride of three months, Liz, over for dinner. They had never met Deek's new wife. His third or fourth, they couldn't remember. Deek was always getting married or at least talking about getting married. But this time it was different; he thought he had hit the mother lode. Deek managed Liz's eighty-acre horse ranch and worked as a horse trainer. He had also opened a roping school and taught team roping to anyone who'd pay him fifty dollars to basically watch him rope steers. Liz had hired Deek to run the ranch because of his knowledge of horses, and for someone to share her bed when she felt the need.

Quinn was always amazed at how Deek, at sixty four, could still sweet-talk the ladies. But it didn't take long to see who the boss was, and it wasn't Deek. Liz was a nice-looking fifty-three-year-old divorcee with a loud dominating personality, and it became obvious from the start that she wanted to be the center of attention. Deek had talked a lot about Quinn and Emma. He had told her how beautiful Emma was, and Liz was surprised at how accurate his description had been. Emma's beauty and style at sixty could hold her own with girls of any age. Her warm and inviting smile, her bright blue eyes could still captivate and hold your attention; you never wanted to look away.

The dinner was planned around Quinn and Deek's next biennial fishing trip to the Bob Marshall Wilderness in North West Montana. They took this trip every two to three years no matter what. This year Quinn had a feeling that it was going to be different from any trip they had taken before. He felt it the minute he met the new bride—things were about to change.

They were all sitting around getting acquainted while Quinn took drink orders. He left them alone and went into the kitchen to make the drinks. On his return, he heard Deek say something he never thought he'd ever hear coming out of Deek's mouth.

"The girls think it would be fun to come along with us this year. What do you think?" Now he was on the spot. What could he say? To Quinn this was the time to get away from life as it came at him and ride his horse through unexplored country just to see what was on the other side of a hill. To fly fish where no one had fished before. To sit around and drink whisky and smoke cigars and just bullshit with his buddy and do nothing. But now, right before his eyes, his old friend had turned the tables on him. Or was it her, his new wife? She had better things in mind for him than to leave her alone while he went off with an old friend to have fun without her. It was all coming clear to him now. This was not something Emma had suggested, although she thought it was great that Quinn wanted her to come along, which is what Deek had told her. Emma's idea of camping out and roughing it was spending a week at the cabin.

"Well, sure, that sounds great, I guess." Quinn had no choice but to go along with them, but he glanced over at Deek with a look that had "you idiot" written all over lt.

So plans were made. In a week Emma and Quinn would pack up their horses and drive to Liz's ranch in Montana. There was only one packhorse, so everyone was limited as to how much they could take along. Quinn gave Emma his large canvas saddlebags. She put her clothes in one side of the bag and her cigarettes in the other. Emma had her priorities, like all smokers—you never want to run out of smokes, especially when you're in the mountains miles away from civilization.

Two days before they were to leave on their trip, about seven in the evening, Emma started to have some pain in her stomach. She got in bed with a heating pad, but the pain only got worse. She asked Quinn to heat some water in a coffee cup, and she held it against her stomach right below her rib cage. This went on for about two hours, until the pain slowly started to subside. In the morning she was exhausted. She had had a gallstone attack, and the stone must have passed through during the night. She had had an attack years before and had refused to go to the hospital. She did the same thing back then, suffered through the pain and said she was fine after the pain was gone. She always said she knew her body and how to take care of most problems when they occurred. What she didn't know was that she could have died from infection.

The next day they started off to Montana. By now Quinn had mellowed out and was glad to see how excited Emma was about the trip. She promised him she would be no trouble and he could still do all the things he loved to do. She told him he might even enjoy having a good cook along for a change.

When they got to Liz's ranch they were all in good spirits, laughing together having fun and getting along like long-lost friends. They went on a quick tour of the ranch. It was a first-class facility. Quinn could've been wrong. Maybe Deek had it right after all. They spent the night and left for the mountains in the morning.

They loaded all the horses and all their gear into Deek's six-horse trailer and started off on a very warm summer day. They drove through Kalispell and onto Highway 2 past Glacier National Park towards the Bob Marshall Wilderness.

Before they arrived at the trailhead they stopped at a small bar tucked away in the woods, miles from anywhere. They went inside and had a beer and a hamburger. This was the last little bit of civilization they would have for the next seven days. As they were leaving the bar, Deek pointed up the road in the direction they were going at a large grizzly bear that was lumbering across the road into the forest next to the trail head. "It looks like we might have some company." Deek said, and they all laughed nervously at the thought. This was grizzly country and they all knew it. They were just a little surprised to see one before they even got on their horses. They drove a mile in on a dirt road and parked the truck, unloaded the horses and got ready for the four to five-hour ride to their camp site. The day went along smoothly, with a lot of joking and laughter as they pushed on further and further into the wilderness.

They set up camp by some trees on the flats just above the rocky shore of the North Fork River. After the long day, Quinn and Emma sat on their sleeping bags in the lean-to they had rigged up and covered with a tarp and watched as Deek set up Liz's large tent with standing head room and two fold-up cots. Emma turned to Quinn. "Now I know why I wasn't allowed to bring more. She might just as well have stayed at home. Do you think they have indoor plumbing?"

Quinn tried to explain that this was not the normal way that he and Deek camped out. They'd never waste time putting up tents. They never spent more than one night in one location before moving on to see what lay ahead. He told her that Deek was just trying to take care of his new bride. He didn't want to rock the boat and fall off the gravy train. Emma loved the lean-to and was glad she had the opportunity to rough it in the wilds with her husband. But the bathroom part was going to take some getting used to. Quinn would give her the .38 revolver, a roll of toilet paper and send her out into the woods to find her own special spot. The .38 was just in case she should come across a bear. The toilet paper was, well, toilet paper.

Everyone was really getting along quite well. Liz and Emma cooked breakfast the first morning and after cleaning up Quinn outfitted her with his fly rod and they set off to the river. Emma took to fly fishing like she did with playing pool. She picked the movement up right away. Quinn would check her line for wind knots. These occur, he explained, when your line goes back over your head then comes forward and crosses inside the line, creating a knot. Most beginners get lots of these knots in their line. There were none in Emma's. She was now starting to sight-fish and beginning to be a show-off with her new-found talent. "Okay, so you picked up the art of fly-fishing, you don't have to be obnoxious about it." Quinn said. He could hardly believe how fast she adapted to the sport.

"I can't help it. This is really fun." Emma replied laughing and smiling. She would see the fish jump and next thing you knew she had snatched it right out of the water. When she hooked up you could hear her excitement as she howled with joy, and it echoed up the river. Emma had found herself a new love.

Each day was filled with new adventures. One day Quinn and Emma decided to take off on foot, just the two of them, and hiked along the creek to where it turned into a heavily wooded forest. Summers are short in the North West, there's July and if you're lucky, part of August and then winter. Pacific storms slide over the Cascades Mountains and across the Yakima Valley into the Rockies. All this rain creates pockets of thick, dense forests throughout the Bob Marshall Wilderness.

The hike was tougher than they expected. They climbed over and around large boulders and crossed through the creek several times. They had to stop often to rest and catch their breath but they continued on. Finally they came to an area of thick trees. It was so lush it almost looked like a rain forest. The trees were tall and cut out much of the sun's light. There were ferns over six feet tall, the grass was up to your knees and moss grew thick on the trees and rocks. It was cool and damp under this canopy of green.

"Now you know why we ride horses." Quinn said, as they sat to rest. They could see a waterfall on the other side of the creek. Emma stretched out in the tall grass and shut her eyes. It was wonderfully peaceful and quiet.

Quinn glanced over at Emma. Her face, framed by the surrounding dark green grass, was lovelier than ever. He gazed upon her long, slender legs and watched as her firm breast rose and fell with each breath. Her beauty had not changed over the years. Her hair was still long and full without a trace of gray. He took his hat off and set it on the ground next to him, then leaned in and kissed her softly on her closed eyes. He lay down next to her on his side as the breeze moved her hair across her face. He reached over with his hand and lifted a lock of hair to the side and kissed her lovingly on the mouth. She put her arm up and pulled him in close and then they kissed each other with a passion that never seemed to grow old.

Caressing her body, Quinn moved his hand to undo her shirt, laid it open then bent down and put his lips to her white stomach. He slowly slid down her jeans and rested his face on her soft mound and took in her scent that aroused his lust and hunger for her that had not diminished but grew with time. This is what they always had, no matter what life threw at them, their love and passion was all they ever needed to exsist on. Emma reached out and touched his head with the tips of her fingers, gently caressed the back of his neck and ran her fingers through his hair. He pulled himself forward as he unbuckled his belt and she opened his shirt; their lips met passionately and their bodies melted together, their hearts pounding as one and arms wrapped tightly around each other. Their hands moving and touching all they could reach, he felt her teeth bite into his lip as their love-making built to a furious pitch and the warmth he felt deep within her came to a boiling climax. Their heavy breathing slowly returning to normal as they lay there with the light shining through the ferns, cast a lacy shadow across their naked bodies…they were to the world as one.

They lay there resting in that cool place. It was so different from where their cabin was. There were no roads here, or cabins or manmade structures; motorized vehicles were prohibited. At their cabin it was never quiet and still like it was here.

They never saw another person the whole time they were in the mountains. They never saw another grizzly bear either. The nights were warm, and sleeping out under the stars made them realize how small and insignificant they were in this enormous universe that God had created. But they felt special too, like this was all put here just for them to enjoy and for no one else. It was their special world now. Emma felt a freedom like she had never felt before. There were no sounds like the still quiet sounds of nature. Emma was enjoying every minute of this new adventure and thinking life could never get any better. And it never did.

On the fourth night after they had their cocktails and dinner of trout, beans and fried potatoes with onions, Emma excused herself and went to bed early. Quinn thought she was just exhausted from being out in the hot sun all day. He went over to see if she needed anything and if she was feeling all right. She said she was fine, just a little tired. Quinn went back and sat by the fire and stayed up talking with Liz and Deek until they turned in for the night. When Quinn walked over to their lean-to, he could tell right away that something was wrong. He bent down on his knees and leaned over Emma. "What's going on? Are you having another gallstone attack?" Emma was in so much pain she couldn't answer. Quinn told her he was going to heat a cup of water on the fire and would be right back. He said nothing to Emma but started thinking about how he was going to ride her out of there and get her to a doctor. When he came back with the hot water, Emma mumbled, "I'm really scared. I think I'm going to die." She was crying in pain. Tears were streaming down her face, "This is so much worse than any of the others."

"I'm going to get Deek and we'll rig something up and get you out of here and to a doctor." He started to leave for Deek's tent.

"No! Don't!" Emma exclaimed. "I don't want them to know. I'm not going to ruin the trip for them."

"But Emma, we can't do anything for you here, and if you die, don't you think that will ruin the trip for them?"

"Just keep heating the water for me. I'll get through it." One thing Quinn knew was once Emma made up her Irish mind there was no changing it. Even if it killed her, she was going to do it her way. Quinn kept the fire going all night and bringing the hot water to her. This went on into the early morning. The pain did finally subside during the night and by the time it was getting light it was over. Emma was so weak and tired she stayed in her sleeping bag and slept until noon. Quinn told them she had a bad night and couldn't sleep. He said she was tired from the hike up the mountain and just needed to rest. When Emma did get up, she had something to eat and then spent the rest of the day lying in the sun on a large flat boulder in the creek that fed into the river. Quinn spent most of the day with her. When they got too hot lying in the sun they would roll off into the cold creek water and then climb back onto the rock. Emma was still distressing from all the pain she went through during the night. Quinn asked her if she thought she could ride her horse out of the mountains tomorrow. She said she was fine and she would have no problem.

The rest of the day went along without a hitch. She slept well that night and felt a hundred percent better by morning. There was still an ache and some soreness but it was manageable. Emma even fixed breakfast for everyone.

It was an abnormally hot summer for that part of the country and around noon they heard the sound of an airplane. They couldn't see it because of the mountains and the trees, but they thought it was strange that it kept circling around and didn't go away. Finally Deek walked out to the river into a clearing to see if he could see where it was. The plane finally showed itself above the mountain in the direction of where their truck and trailer were parked. Deek knew right away what was going on. Quinn walked over where Deek was standing and looked up at the plane, "Isn't that one of those fire-fighting planes that drops that red fire deterrent on forest fires?"

"Yep, that's what it is alright."

"Well, shit, man, we should probably pack up and get the hell out of here." Quinn said. He was mainly concerned about Emma's health and her ability to ride out if they got in a real jam. There were no signs of any fire and they couldn't smell or see any smoke but it gave him a good excuse to get Emma out of the mountains and home to a doctor.

They all seemed to think it was a good idea and they were going to leave the next morning anyway. Besides, they were running out of food and booze. Emma had no problems riding all the way back to where they had parked the truck. Actually she was feeling really good and after they loaded the horses in the trailer and were driving out she suggested stopping at that little bar for a beer and a hamburger, which they did.

As they drove out of the mountains they could look back and see the smoke from the fire. It looked to be somewhere in the Glacier Park area.

Two days later after they returned home Emma said she wanted to go to the cabin for a few days. She craved to recapture the feelings she felt when she was up in the wilderness. It was hard to get back to normal after being alone in the solitude of the wilderness.

Traffic and people and all the sounds of civilization seemed much louder now. It was going to take time to adjust to the real world.

Quinn said he would take her to the cabin, but first she had to see the doctor. Emma argued that she was fine now and there was no reason to see a doctor. Quinn said she was always fine before an attack but they were happening more frequently now and he didn't want to go through that again. It was too hard on him to watch her suffer like that. If you won't do it for yourself, at least do it for me, he told her.

The only appointment she could get before the weekend was late Friday afternoon. Emma talked Quinn into packing everything so they could leave for the cabin right after her doctor's appointment. Quinn did as she asked, knowing that when Emma sets her mind on something it becomes virtually impossible to change it.

While they sat in the waiting room waiting for the doctor, Emma was getting anxious and kept insisting, "We're just wasting time when we should be on the road."

The nurse finally called them into the examining room to wait some more. Ten minutes later the doctor came in. After Emma told him about her problems, he had her lie back on the table and he pushed his hands in different spots on her stomach. He touched on one spot that caused instant pain, to Emma's surprise, and she winced in discomfort. Emma had told the doctor of their plans of leaving his office and driving directly to their cabin in the mountains. His reply was, "The only place you're going is to the hospital." Emma was out of arguments. Quinn checked her into the hospital and drove home, unloaded the truck and drove back.

In the morning the doctor preformed an endoscopy to see what exactly was going on and to remove any stones that might still be lodged in her gall bladder. The news was not good. What the doctor had discovered was much more than just a gall bladder that had to be removed. As he was removing his camera from inside Emma's stomach he noticed a troubling sight in her esophagus and upper stomach. The trip to the doctors turned out to be a trip to hell. Emma had esophageal carcinoma and stomach cancer. This was when Quinn heard that word for the first time and never again. Emma never heard it at all. TERMINAL.

# CHAPTER THREE

It was still dark and beginning to rain again. There's never a lot of traffic at this hour, which was a comfort to Quinn's aging eyesight. He finally had to confess about his night vision; it was getting worse and over the past few years he never quite felt comfortable driving at night. The tears that now rolled down his cheeks were more than tears of sorrow but tears that came, he believed, from allergies along with age. Quinn wiped away the moisture that blurred his vision with his fingers while concentrating on the white lines in the road; the broken lines that began to resemble the flipping of cards as they disappeared past the truck, one after the other.

He kept thinking of Emma. He remembered seeing her for the first time. It was during a spring roundup. He couldn't take his eyes off of her. There was something familiar about her. Emma was very pretty, but it was much more than her beautiful face. He felt he knew her from somewhere, in another place or another time. It was a strange feeling he couldn't explain.

He remembered when Emma told him what she remembered about their first meeting.

"It was at the branding, and you kept staring at me all day."

"No, I didn't." Quinn said, still trying to be cool.

"Yes, you did, and I was staring at you too. When I first saw you standing with your friends, my heart stopped beating. I thought to myself, oh my God that's him. That's the man I'm going to marry. He's the man I've been dreaming about. You were tall with black hair and olive skin. The way you looked at me with those amazing brown black eyes and the most handsome chiseled face I'd ever seen. I knew you knew me also and someday you'd be mine and we'd get married." Emma was only eighteen but she was certain this would come to pass.

His thoughts were interrupted by a large semi that flew by at a high rate of speed, creating a foggy mist that obscured his view. Startled out of his day dream, he was driving blind now and couldn't see any part of the road. Quinn held his breath. He squeezed the steering wheel tight with both hands and leaned forward to try and find the road. He slowed down, letting the semi put distance between them. As the fog began to clear, he sat back and took a deep breath. Shaken, he began thinking about getting off the interstate and taking the old road. After over an hour of light traffic the highway was filling up with morning commuters. The traffic was getting heavy and it was still raining. Hardly any cars traveled the old road anymore and never any large trucks. It would take him longer but he'd feel more at ease. After all, he wasn't on any time schedule and he sure wasn't in any hurry.

Quinn got off the interstate at the next off ramp and drove three miles to the old road and stopped at the intersection. Now this I can handle, he thought. Checking in both directions, there were no signs of cars coming or going. He turned onto the old road and started off again, feeling more confident. The road had been neglected over the years, ever since they built the interstate. It wasn't in very good condition, but he didn't care as long as there wasn't any traffic.

Even with the rain, it felt peaceful being the only person on this deserted road. He drove past farm houses where lights were just now coming on as their day was about to begin. He drove past open fields and followed the road as it curved along the natural lay of the land.

Past events returned to him and his comfort level grew. He was relaxing and started remembering again.

It was Emma's birthday. She was twenty-five and she was not happy. "I just wanted it to be special, that's all." Emma said.

Quinn raised his hand and tenderly touched her cheek. "I know, and I did too." Dropping his arm, he held her hands and said, "But I can't help it. They're coming in tonight and I promised I would pick them up at the airport. We always have a great time with them. It will be fun, you'll see."

"But we never get to be alone anymore. Then when we finally get a baby sitter, we have to share our time with other people."

"I'm sorry honey. I promise I'll make it up to you."

"You know with the kids around it's hard to find time just for us." Emma was becoming discouraged and feeling neglected.

"It's your favorite restaurant." Quinn said trying to make things sound more rewarding.

"It's not the food that matters. I just had it all planned differently. It's turning out to be a really crappy birthday." She started to pout.

"Now don't be like that."

"Easy for you to say, it's not your birthday."

They drove to the airport in virtual silence. Not even a glance in each other's direction. Emma reached over and turned on the radio, Waylon Jennings was singing his latest hit song, "Amanda." Quinn started to say something and Emma reached over and turned the radio up louder. They went on in silence. He pulled into the parking lot, stopped the car and got out. Emma wasn't moving.

"Come on, honey," he said.

"No, I'll wait here."

"No, you come in with me, and stop being silly."

"Alright, but I'm really ..."She stopped in mid-sentence, got out and slammed the car door.

They went inside the terminal and started walking towards the gate.

"Come on, hurry," he said, rushing along

"What's the hurry? They can only come out one way. There's no way we could miss them," Emma said, trying to keep up with him.

"Quinn, the people are getting on the plane, not off. Are you sure you have the arrival time right?"

"I think so; let's see if they're still on the plane."

"Wait, we can't go on the plane."

"Yes, we can."

"No, they won't let us."

"Oh, yes they will. I have two tickets that say we can get on this plane. Happy birthday honey, we're going to Hawaii, just the two of us."

"Is this a joke?"

"No, look, here are the tickets." Quinn waved the tickets in front of her to prove it to her. Emma had a bewildered look on her face.

"I don't believe you. You're kidding me? How did you manage to do this? What about my clothes?"

"You're not going need any clothes where we're going. But your mom and Kim did pack a few things for you and brought them to the airport earlier and picked up the tickets and checked us in."

With that she began to cry. "I can't believe you did this. I had no idea," she said, as the tears of joy started flowing down her cheeks. She threw her arms around his neck and began kissing him.

"I love you and I feel so guilty. I've been mean to everyone today. I've been such a spoiled brat. Are you sure about this?"

"Yes, you have been a spoiled brat and, yes, I almost canceled it twice. But we're still going and believe me, we're going to have a great time. You deserve this." Emma had spent the entire summer planning and putting on her friend Kim's wedding and like she always did, gave a hundred percent.

"What about the girls?"

"Your mom has it all worked out, and Kim said she'd help her with the kids. You don't have to worry, they'll be fine."

He was jolted out of his day dream as a large yellow sign comes into view with only one word on it, DIP. And as soon as the word registered in his head, the sound of the road was gone, the wheels spun freely and it felt like he was floating; then his rig came crashing down, sparks flew out from under the trailer with a screeching sound of metal dragging along the blacktop. His body flung forward then back, smashing his head against the rear window. Sugar was thrown up in the air, hit the roof of the cab and landed at his feet. Looking in the rear view mirror he saw the trailer going from one side of the truck to the other. The trailer came loose and Bracket was back there getting knocked around. He slowed down, trying to keep the trailer behind him so it wouldn't go off the road and roll over. There was a loud bang as the trailer hit the back of the truck and bounced off to one side. I've got to keep it behind the truck and slow it down, he kept saying to himself. Slowing he kept maneuvering his truck to keep the trailer in sight as it banged into the truck and pulled back and banged into it again, until finally he was able to pull to a stop off to the side of the road.

He took a deep breath. His hands were damp with sweat. He was squeezing the steering wheel so tight that the skin on his knuckles was about to split open. "Shit, what the hell happened?" he said as he turned to Sugar. "Girl, are you alright?" Sugar jumped back up onto the seat and sat staring at him. He reached over and touched her on the head. Then picked her up and held her in his arms. "You seem to be okay. You stay here while I go check on Bracket."

Quinn stepped out of the truck and into the rain that was now coming down in a steady drizzle. He walked back to the trailer and opened the side door to look inside. It was dark. He could smell Bracket's warm breath but could barely see him. "How's it going in there boy?" he whispered. The big bay stuck his head out and looked at him with large intelligent eyes. His nostrils flared as he nuzzled up against Quinn's hand. Quinn saw blood running down his forehead. There was also a small cut on his lip. "I'll be back in a minute and get you out of there."

He moved to the front of the trailer and got down on his hands and knees and looked under the truck to inspect the damage. The trailer hitch had broken loose on one side and fallen to the ground, but the other side was still attached. The trailer's jack assembly had busted off when it came down hard on the street. Now he couldn't unhitch the trailer and he couldn't drive the truck because the hitch was still attached on one side.

Quinn knew he was in a real dilemma. Well, first things first. He had to get Bracket out of the trailer and check him out thoroughly before doing anything else. There was one more problem. The trailer was now tilted forward at an angle. The tongue was bent and lying on the ground and the back of the trailer was pointing upward. There was no way Bracket could back out. He walked around and opened the double doors of the trailer. There was an overwhelming aroma of horse sweat. That must have scared the hell out of him, he thought. Bracket was standing in a downward angle facing forward. He was going to have to turn him around in order to get him out.

The wind was blowing the rain into the open end of the trailer. It was still dark outside and pitch-black inside the trailer. Quinn climbed in to remove the four pins that held the divider in place. The floor mats were cold and wet, with a distinct odor of fresh horseshit. Bracket kept moving his feet up and down in a nervous dance. "It's going to be okay, boy. I'll get you out of here. You'll be fine, just fine." Quinn kept talking to him in a soothing voice as he slowly removed the pins. He pulled the divider out of the trailer and set it outside on the ground. He grabbed hold of the halter next to Bracket's cheek and slowly turned his head to the side, talking softly, trying to keep him relaxed. He needed to convince Bracket that what he was doing was best for him.

Little by little he began to turn the horse around. Bracket seemed to sense what had to be done. At one point during the turn-around, it got so cramped, Quinn was getting crushed between the horse and the inside wall of the trailer. After numerous tries he finally had Bracket turned around and facing out the back of the trailer.

Now, Bracket was going to have to jump out. Quinn went around behind his horse to push him forward. "Okay boy, it's up to you. This is the only way out of here." Then he slapped him on the butt as hard as he could and yelled "Jump!" Bracket started to brace himself, then he hesitated. His feet started dancing nervously again. "Try it again, boy. Jump!" Quinn shouted louder this time as he slapped him on the butt. Bracket leaped forward out of the trailer and as he was landing, he slipped on the wet pavement and went down on his knees. Then he quickly scrambled back up and took off running.

Quinn watched the horse as he disappeared from view into the dark misty night. The wind and the drizzling rain were blowing in his face as he stared down the road. Quinn climbed out of the trailer with the lead line in hand and started walking after him. He had walked about a quarter mile before he finally caught a glimpse of his horse. He was eating grass alongside of the road. That's a good sign, Quinn thought. He's acting like nothing's happened.

He walked up to Bracket and clipped the lead line onto the halter, and as he was walking him back, he kept listening to the sound of his hoofs on the pavement to see if there was any unusual rhythm to his gait. It was still dark, and he couldn't see if he was limping or not. Bracket's head held still and didn't bob with each step and from what Quinn could hear, he seemed to be fine. When he got back to the truck, he went around to the side of the trailer and tied him to a tie ring.

He opened the passenger side door and started rummaging through the glove box until he finally found the flashlight. He walked back to the trailer where he had tied Bracket and inspected the injuries to his head. There was a large gash on his forehead above his right eye. It was a fairly deep cut. Quinn cleaned that wound first. The cut on the lip had already stopped bleeding. He wasn't going to worry about that one. There was one more scrape on his right knee where he landed on the pavement after jumping from the trailer. That one didn't look too bad either but he'd keep an eye on it. Bracket seemed to be in pretty good shape. While walking back to the trailer there hadn't seemed to be a sign of him limping. His legs must be all right, especially after the way he took off running.

Discouraged, Quinn moved slowly back to his truck, opened the door and sat down. He reached over and picked up Sugar and held her on his lap. Looking out into the dark night, he said, "So Emma, what am I going to do now?" His voice trailed off. "I don't have a lot of choices, do I?" He could sit here and wait for someone to come by and help. But he hadn't seen one car since they turned onto the old road. He couldn't just leave his horse tied to the trailer and go off looking for help, and waiting around wasn't something he did well. So what was left? He knew the town of Melville was up ahead about five or six miles. He couldn't drive there, so he decided to ride.

Quinn pulled his saddle out of the trailer, laid a pad on Bracket's back, slung the saddle up and rocked it in place then tightened the cinch. He slid the bit into Bracket's mouth and adjusted the headstall, then led him up to the truck. He brought his saddlebags out and tied them securely on his saddle. There was still a light drizzle coming down so he slipped into his rain slicker. He tied a bedroll on the back of his saddle and took the canvas bag of grain and hung it over the saddle horn. He also put a few cans of dog food into his saddlebags. That was about all he could manage for now; he had no idea how or when he'd get back to his truck. He locked the truck and put the keys in his pocket. He picked up Sugar and mounted his horse and started off into the cold dark night, riding towards the small town of Melville.

The rain started to come down hard again and in the dark it was difficult to see the road in front of him. He thought he heard something off in the distance and stopped his horse to listen. There it was, he could hear the whispering again somewhere out in the darkness. He turned his head to listen but then thought it was just the wind blowing through the scattered patches of juniper. He listened again and then put it out of his mind and moved on.

Quinn looked down at Sugar. The rain was dripping off the brim of his hat onto her nose. She kept shaking her head and licking at the drops as they landed. He slid her back into his slicker and covered her to make her more comfortable. Sugar was not an outdoor kind of dog. Emma had purchased her one night on the

Internet.  It was right after her cancer surgery, and she was pretty well drugged up at the time.  She said she needed a companion dog to keep her company.  Sugar was an expensive Maltese with long white hair that parted down the middle of her back.  Quinn had known nothing of Emma's purchase until the dog arrived at the airport and he had to go pick her up.  But what could he say?  After all, Emma had bought him a very expensive horse, and besides the dog turned out to be a blessing.  Sugar would lie next to her day and night and comfort her while bolstering her spirits.  Quinn thought she was one of the smartest dogs he'd ever known.

They were riding alongside this quiet road with no traffic.  He still hadn't seen a car all night.  After hitting that dip it's no wonder there were no cars, he thought, only an idiot would drive this road at night, an idiot like me.

They had been on the move for about thirty minutes, and it was just now starting to get light.  Quinn decided to ride up on a hill above the road to see if he could see the lights of the town from a higher vantage point.  The rain began to let up and the air felt heavy in the cold mist.

When they reached the top of the hill, he looked out over the land.  The sky was now a dark steel gray and a thin bright glow appeared on the horizon above the hills to the east.  Out in the distance, he could see the lights of the town.  Quinn sat on his horse and looked off to the west where a steady stream of headlights moved across the valley floor, maybe three miles away.  As the highway made a sweeping bend to the north, the lights turned red.

They started back down the hill in the direction of the town.  Ever since the interstate highway went through this small farming town at the base of the mountains had been dying on the vine.  But there was still one major investor left in town, Mr. McDonald.

They rode over the first rise, and from there he could see it, lighting up the sky in its bright reds and yellows, and through the cold mist, it welcomed them into town, the Golden Arches.  They rode on as it coaxed them forward.  By the time they arrived in front of the McDonalds, the rain had stopped and the sun was peeking over the distant hills, giving the land a fresh bright sheen.

# CHAPTER FOUR

The McDonalds was just opening up for the day, and Quinn could smell the salt and hot grease from the street. He walked Bracket into the drive-thru lane and stopped at the outside speaker to place his order — egg McMuffin, a large black coffee and a side order of bacon—without getting off his horse, then rode around to the window to claim his breakfast. He paid the girl at the window and took the brown paper bag with his food, gesturing a thanks with a nod of his head and a touch to the brim of his hat.

Quinn rode out toward the street where he saw some picnic tables and benches near a creek just past the restaurant. He rode over, got off his horse and set Sugar on the ground. Then he loosened the latigo on the saddle and took the bridle off Bracket, so he could graze on the grass that grew near the creek. He picked up Sugar and sat her on top of the table and fed her the bacon while he sat down straddling the bench to drink his coffee and think about the day ahead. He devoured the egg McMuffin without even tasting it. His thoughts were not on food.

As he stared down at the ground in front of him, his mind kept drifting back to Emma and the promises he'd made to her. He was having a hard time concentrating on the problem at hand. He wasn't thinking straight and he knew it, and yet he had to deal with this new situation that had been thrust upon him. Things were not going as planned and he had no one to help him, and right then he didn't want to deal with the sadness that kept flowing over him like ocean waves one after another. He didn't know anyone in this small town he was stuck in, but he had to find some way to repair his damaged truck and trailer.

Quinn sat at the table and removed the wild rag from around his heck. He took the three-foot square scarf and folded it into a triangle, then tied the two corners together making a sling. He slipped it over his head, hoping the large scarf would help support Sugar while they were riding.

When they had finished eating, Quinn walked over and got Bracket and put his bridle on and tightened the cinch. He picked up Sugar, climbed into the saddle and adjusted the little dog in the new sling. Sugar took to it right away and seemed more at ease. Quinn turned Bracket towards town and headed into the unknown. It was still early and this small forgotten burg seemed deserted. There was an eerie quietness about it. The only sounds were the creaking of the saddle and the rhythm of Bracket's hoofs tapped out a steady beat on the pavement. They moved slowly along the main street with small houses scattered about. Quinn looked over his shoulder when he heard a car approaching from the rear. The car slowed down letting the driver have a better look at this stranger on the horse, then sped away. At one point a dog ran out from somewhere and started barking at Bracket's heels. Sugar looked back at the large angry dog and answered with a high-pitched bark of her own, which startled the dog and he stopped, then turned and walked away.

They continued on, leaving the residential part of town and entering more of the business section. Quinn spotted a building at the end of a side street that had old cars parked in its back lot.

He turned his horse and rode down to the end of the street to take a better look. It was a small metal building set back from the street with a gravel parking lot out front; it looked like a wrecking yard and hopefully an auto shop. The parking lot was empty, and there didn't seem to be anyone around. Quinn got off his horse, walked over and looked inside through a window in the front of the building. It was some kind of a business establishment, but no hours were posted.

He got on his horse and rode back to the main street and continued on into town. About three blocks up they came to a small motel, probably built in the late forties. As they got closer, he spotted two pipe stalls behind the motel. He stopped Bracket in front of the motel, dismounted and tied him to one of the posts holding a sign, "Sweet Dreams Motel." That was something he hadn't had in a long time. Maybe it's an omen of things to come. He took Sugar in his arms and walked up the steps to the office and went inside. It was a tiny office with a counter and behind the counter there was an open door that led to living quarters. Sitting in a chair behind the counter was an elderly man watching a small television. He glanced up as Quinn walked in. "I'll be right with you," the man said. He seemed pissed off at something and kept changing channels.

Finally in disgust he turned it off. "Nothing but crap during the day. Anyway; what can I do for you?"

"I see you have some pipe stalls in the back. Are they for rent?"

"With a room they're free."

"That's great; my truck broke down outside of town. The dog and I rode in on my horse." Quinn explained, as the man glanced over his shoulder at Bracket tied to his sign out front.

"That's a bit of bad luck."

"Yeah, I've had a bit of that lately. I'm looking for a mechanic, someone with a tow truck."

"Well, we have a pretty good mechanic in town, but I think they're closed today but they should be open tomorrow. It's at the end of cedar street, you can't miss it. They'll be able to help you."

"Okay, move me in, and I'll put my horse in one of your pipe stalls."

"Fill out this card and we'll get you all set up."

"Is it alright with the dog?"

"Sure, that's no problem."

"Is there any hay and water back there?"

"Yeah, the hay is under a tarp. You can throw him a couple flakes and I'll just put it on your bill."

"Thanks." Quinn started to walk out.

"Hey, don't you want your key? It's room four."

"Oh, yeah, I'm not thinking too clear this morning I've been up all night."

Quinn walked his horse around to the back of the motel. There were two old rusty pipe stalls that looked like they hadn't been used for some time. Weeds were growing in them and they hadn't been very well-maintained. Bracket should be fine for a day or two and hopefully not much longer. He pulled the tarp back to check the hay and just as he lifted up the tarp, a black chicken jumped out and startled him. It almost knocked him over before scurrying off. He looked back down at the bale of hay and there were two brown eggs sitting there. He picked them up and put them in his jacket pocket. They were still warm. The hay was in surprisingly good condition, considering it was also being used as a chicken coop.

Quinn took off his saddlebags and unsaddled Bracket. He put the saddle on a bale of hay and gave two flakes to Bracket, then covered up his saddle and the hay with the tarp. The water looked good and clean and there was plenty of it. He shut the gate to the stall and walked back to the office. When he walked in the old man stood up and asked if everything was all right. "Yeah, fine, I just brought you two eggs I found in your hay."

"Thanks, they're from that old black hen. She's so damn old now I thought she'd gone dry. There's not much left inside them shells, but she's still trying." Quinn smiled at the old man and walked back out to find his room, Sugar following close behind.

As Quinn opened the door there was a musty smell that said this room hadn't been used in a long time. He left the door open and went over and opened a window to help air it out. It's a wonder there aren't weeds growing in here too, he thought. It was a small room, but besides the smell from being closed up, it looked clean. There was a neatly made double bed, a TV, a sofa against one wall and a chair next to the bathroom door.

Quinn was exhausted from the day's events and it wasn't even noon yet. His aching body was trying to tell him he had already put in a full day. He'd been up and going for more than twelve hours. It was no wonder his body and mind felt drained. He hadn't realized, with all he'd been through, that it was now catching up to him. He just thought it was the same old tired feeling he had been experiencing lately.

Quinn hung the saddle bags over the back of the chair, walked over and sat on the bed, pulled off his boots and dropped them on the floor. He grabbed a pillow from under the bedspread, fluffed it up and stretched out on the bed with his hat over his eyes. Sugar jumped up next to him and made herself comfortable. "We'll just lie here for a few minutes and gather our thoughts, then go see what this town has to offer." Quinn mumbled to Sugar as his eye lids became heavy and they both went right to sleep. It was early evening when his heart started racing and he could hear the voice whispering. It woke him up. It must be another dream, he thought. He's had these dreams before, but they seem to be happening more often. Quinn sat up on the edge of the bed and yawned and rubbed his eyes then reached down, picked up his boots and put them on. He called to Sugar and she followed him outside.

They made their way around to back of the motel to give Bracket some grain and examined the cuts on his face. They seemed to be healing fine.

40

When Quinn was younger, working on their ranch, he had always looked at a horse like just another piece of ranch equipment. He never cared what horse he was on as long as it could get the job done. Horses were a necessary part of a ranch's operation. Older now and riding the same horse for the last several years, he'd bonded with Bracket. They'd become like buddies or friends. It would be another sad day in his life if he were to lose him. He brushed and groomed Bracket before walking back to the front of the motel.

The town had come to life. There were cars in the street and people walking on the sidewalks. Quinn stood observing them as they went about their business; it all had an aura of being terminal. Most of the people seemed to be just trying to outlive the town. It was all they'd ever known, and once the town was gone, there would be no place for them.

Quinn noticed there was a bar, one block up, on the other side of the street. A beer sounded good to him right about now, so he picked up Sugar and started across the street towards the local watering hole, glancing in the shop windows as he walked along. Many of them were closed and appeared like they'd been closed for some time, their windows filthy with dust piling up on their sills. When he reached the bar he looked up at the neon sign over the door. It kept flickering on and off and making loud buzzing sounds. It was called The Moose Head Bar & Grill. The door to the bar had a small round window in it. He peeked in. It looked empty. He tried the door. It opened, so he went in.

It was a long, narrow room with a four-quarter pool table in the back. The bar was on the right as you walked in. Lined up in front of the bar, were eight maroon vinyl padded barstools, some of which had been repaired with duct tape. Above the bar was an old worn and dusty moose head with cobwebs draped from the antlers… that probably accounted for the name. There were two large ornately framed dusty mirrors on either side of the moose head. And in front of the mirrors were two stuffed rattlesnakes. Quinn thought the name Rattlesnake Bar & Grill sounded more interesting.

Quinn stepped up to the bar and ordered a beer. "How's business these days?" He was trying to be friendly. It never hurt to have a bartender as a friend. The bartender was a tall thin man in his early sixties with a ridge of gray hair around a balding head. He had a large, faded tattoo on his left forearm that might have been a dragon at one time. Quinn thought he probable got it in Vietnam.

"It's always slow this time of day, it'll pick up, drinkers like to drink,"

"Is it okay with my dog? I'll keep a tight hand on her."

"Oh, sure, as long as she's drinking," the bartender chuckled.

Quinn smiled, "We'll split a beer. What's on the grill?"

"Oh, there hasn't been a grill in here in years, ever since the fire. We had no insurance at the time. I never got around to changing the sign and I can't afford to fix the kitchen. It's just a little bit of false advertising. I've got some mini pretzels."

Quinn took the pretzels and his beer and went over to a small table against the wall close to the pool table and sat Sugar in a chair. He remained standing while he broke a pretzel and gave it to Sugar, then sauntered over to the pool table. He moved slowly around the table, dragging his fingers along the felt. The felt was old and worn with cigarette burns on the rails and a slight tear down the center.

It seemed like yesterday when he and Emma had played pool in places just like this, and she could play pretty good pool, too. She had amazing hand-eye coordination. She could beat him four out of five games. They'd dance to an old jukebox, like the one in the corner, too. Emma always wanted to lead. She would say "You're off beat," and then she'd count in his ear, quick quick slow, quick quick slow, over and over until he got back in step. She always moved with such ease and control, she loved to dance. There were times when she could out ride him on her horse too. But she couldn't out live him. His thoughts trailed off... We were really something.

He went back to the table, sat down in the chair next to Sugar and looked around the room. There was one other person in the bar besides himself that he hadn't noticed when he first walked in. From where he sat she looked like a middle-aged woman, and she was sitting at the end of the bar, next to the front door. He watched her for a few moments, and then like her, he turned his head and stared at the beer that sat in front of him. He felt empty inside.

After a while the bartender brought him another beer and asked if he was all right. "Yeah, I'm fine... thanks." Quinn had lost all sense of time; it seemed like hours before anyone else came into the bar. Quinn heard the door open and he looked up as three young men, who looked to be in their late twenties, and a young girl with piercings and oddly cut and colored hair, all came in together. By the looks of them, they had already started their drinking. Quinn doesn't know them but he knows their kind; loud, self-centered and disrespectful of others, and worst of all a sense of entitlement. They stopped at the bar for beers, then headed back to the pool table. The biggest and oldest-looking of the three, tells his friend, who he calls "Tithead"...

"Rack 'em, so I can kick your ass."

"I always put up the money, when is it your turn?"

"Well, when you win I'll put the fucking money in. Hey, babe, go get us some more beers, okay?"

Quinn kept staring at the pool table as their talking and laughing got louder. The big guy reminded him of a pool game years ago, before he and Emma had children. They were up in Billings, Montana, at an open-consignment horse sale. They left without making a purchase and were driving home with an empty trailer and decided to stop at a little beer joint out side of town for a bite to eat. The bar had a couple of pool tables in the back, and they were going strong. On the wall was a chalkboard, and to play you signed in and waited your turn. They sat down at a small table and ordered. Emma got up and strolled back to chalkboard and wrote her name.

They'd just finish eating and were walking out the door when the bartender called out her name. Emma stopped and looked up at Quinn, smiled, shrugged her shoulders, and hurried back to the pool table to pick out a cue stick from the rack. He followed her inside and stopped at the bar, ordered another beer and sat on a stool to watch. She rolled her stick on the table to see how straight it was and inserted four quarters into the coin slot than released the balls and racked them. Emma at times could play good pool. She had an eye for the game, but her first game always seemed to be her best, and then she'd lose her concentration and rush her shots. The guy she was playing had his own personal cue stick, which he carried in a black satchel. He set the satchel on the table and clicked open the snaps and removed the two sections and screwed them together. He was ready to play.

"He's a real jerk," the bartender whispered to Quinn, "and also the best player in town,"

The game started with his break. When it was Emma's turn, she walked slowly around the table, looking for her best shot. She'd always lean over real slow and toss her dark auburn hair to one side before taking her shot. She looked hot, and she knew it. She used her looks to her advantage, which often threw her male opponents off their game.

She played him, even up to the last. The 8 ball was against the rail at one end of the table and the cue ball was against the rail at the other end of the table. It was a difficult shot for any player. Emma tapped the pocket next to the cue ball with her stick to indicate where she intended the 8 ball to end up. She brushed her hair aside with her hand and leaned in for her shot then gave a little shake of her booty, just to punctuate her confidence. She hit the 8 ball hard, just right, and it came screaming back up the rail to the pocket. Game over. It was one hell of a shot.

It was then that Quinn decided it was time to leave. The crowd was full of locals annoyed at the idea of a young pretty girl and an outsider coming into their bar and embarrassing their best player. Quinn took Emma's hand and they slipped out into the parking lot. He put his arm over Emma's shoulder and she put her arm around his waist as they laughed and hooted over Emma's victory. They were young and in love and felt invincible.

They laughed a lot in those days. Laughter was always there in their lives. They believed in laughter, and laughter helped keep Emma alive through the years of her illness. But the laughter was gone now. Emma took it with her. Quinn couldn't remember the last time he had a good laugh or saw much humor in anything. Everything had changed. The laughter had soured into sadness and he didn't want to live like this but he had no control now over his emotions.

"Hey, damn it! I told you to get us another beer. Shit, what the fuck are you doing?"

Quinn turned to face the angry sound that filled the room and what he saw was darkness and contempt. He looked away quickly and took a swallow of beer then glanced back as the young girl slid from her chair and began working her way towards the bar. When she reached his table she stopped and looked down at Sugar.

"What kind of a dog is that?" She asked.

"She's a Maltese."

"What's her name?"

"Sugar."

"That's really a cute name."

"Get the damn beers," echoed again through the bar. She turned and hurried off. A moment later she was on her way back with the beers and set them on the table next to all the empties. She took a beer, sat down and watched them play for a while, her fingernail picking at the label on the beer bottle. "Babe, watch me make this tricky shot." She stood up for a better view. "How about that, was that a fucking great shot or what?"

"That was real good, Lloyd." She said without any emotion and sat back down.

"Yeah, it was. Okay Tithead, rack 'em up."

She looked over at the old man and his dog and moved over to their table and sat in a chair next to the dog. "Can I hold her?" she asked.

"Sure, she likes being held. She was my wife's dog, a companion while she was sick. Now it's just me and Sugar."

Suddenly a pool stick came flying across the room and landed right next to Quinn's chair. Quinn's natural reaction was to reach down and retrieve it for the player, but as soon as he put his fingers around the pool stick Lloyd was there to stomp on it crushing Quinn's fingers, and holding them pinned to the floor. The burning pain is intense and rushes up his arm into his shoulder. It felt like the bones in his fingers were breaking as beads of sweat formed on his forehead.

Then he heard that angry voice, "Give me that fucking little mutt. I'm getting rid of it. The stinking shit doesn't belong in a bar."

"It was his wife's dog and she's dead," the girl pleaded.

"Well, it'll soon be following right after her. Now give it to me."

Sugar growls as Lloyd grabs her by the throat, but when he reaches over for the dog, he steps forward taking his foot off the pool stick and stands with one foot on either side and at that precise instant, Quinn rams the pool stick up between Lloyd's legs; cracking him in the testicles like the snap of a bullwhip. Lloyd legs buckle as the air is sucked from his lungs, he gasped and bends over the table bracing himself with his hand while trying to catch his breath and releases his grip on Sugar, and before he can recover, Quinn chokes up on the cue stick, like a baseball bat, and without hesitating, and in one violent blow brings it crashing down on Lloyd's head, striking him behind the ear, slamming his face onto the table as blood spurts out from beneath his head. Lloyd's knees give way as his bloody face drags across the table before collapsing onto the floor unconscious.

The scene is surreal in the now silence of the room. Blood is everywhere. Lloyd's friends just stood there in disbelief, shocked at their feared leader crumpled on the floor in front of them. The girl draws a quick breath, her mouth half open, looks on in a blank stare, unable to weigh the sight before her eyes. Quinn doesn't stick around. He snatches the dog from the girl's arms, and backs away from the table, then turns around and walks up to the bartender. "Can you sell me a bottle of whiskey?"

"I sure can."

"And maybe a little bag of ice."

"No problem."

"I'll come by in the morning to see if there are damages you want me to pay for."

"There won't be any damages to worry about. That asshole has been looking for trouble for a long time. It's about time somebody gave him his comeuppance. Thanks for the entertainment."

Quinn took the bottle of whiskey and bag of ice, and with his dog under one arm, he walked out of the bar and across the street to the motel.

# CHAPTER FIVE

Quinn walked across the street feeling no fear. There was nothing to be afraid of. He didn't care what happened. He had been wound like a tight spring, and was glad he could release all the anger festering inside him. There was nothing anyone could do to hurt him anymore. He welcomed all comers.

Inside his motel room, he picked up a glass in the bathroom and poured it half full with whiskey. He took the glass, the bottle and the bag of ice and went over and sat on the bed. He took his boots off, dropped them on the floor and put his hand in the bag of ice while he drank the whiskey. His fingers were throbbing, but the ice eased the pain. He sat there looking out through the space between the drapes at the town's few lights, drinking whiskey and tried to remember what had just happened. It all went by so fast. The blood he remembered, the blood and taking Sugar and walking out of the bar. But the rest was just a blur.

He finally got up and went to the bathroom, and when he came out he had his shirt and pants off. He set them on the chair and climbed into bed. Sugar jumped up on the bed next to him like she always did. It was still and quiet in the room. He set the glass on the table, closed his eyes and began to drift off into a strange dream. He was sitting on the floor in the corner of a small room. Three strange men were standing over him, asking him questions. They asked him about living and dying, and he didn't know what to say. They asked if he had ever died before, and he shook his head. They put him inside a wooden box and told him to try to remember. He looked up and saw the light disappear as the lid was put in place. Then he heard someone nailing the lid on. He could hear the hammer, bang, bang, bang. "I can't remember," he said. It was hard to breathe. His heart was pounding as the hammering continued. He forced his eyes open. There was no box and no sound. It wasn't the whispering voice this time. He lay still and waited and listened. There it was again. It was a knocking sound that woke him up. The door, he thought, there is someone at the door. He sat up, a little

47

startled. Who could be knocking on his door? No one knew he was here.

"What?" he said in a loud voice. "Who is it?"

"It's me."

"Who the hell is "me"?"

"It's me, Jodi, from the bar."

He didn't say anything.

"You remember. I was talking to you and you let me hold your dog."

"Yeah, what do you want?"

"I'm scared, I'm really scared," she said. "Can I come in?"

He felt awkward and wasn't sure what to say. "Are you alone?"

"Yes."

Quinn got to his feet and put his pants on and walked over to the door, hesitating for a moment, not wanting to deal with it, and then he opened the door. She stood there, trembling; then looked back up the street as if to make sure no one was watching.

Quinn could tell she was upset. "Well, who are you scared of?"

"Lloyd, the guy you busted up tonight."

"Where is he?"

"I don't know. His two friends put him in his car and took him somewhere. When you left the bar, I followed you outside and saw you walk over here."

Quinn looked outside, over her shoulder, to see if anyone else was out there. She seemed to be alone. He stood in front of her at the door, looking down at her. He knew this was against his better judgment, but he finally said, "Alright, come on in."

"Gee, thanks. He's really got me scared. I think he's going to beat me up now."

"Why would he do that?"

"He just will, I know him."

"What reason could he have to hurt you?"

"Just because he can, that's why."

"That doesn't make any sense."

"I was talking to you and playing with your dog. He can get real mad, and he's really going to be mad once he recovers from what you did to him."

She was a plain, skinny girl about five four. Her hair was chopped short and colored with bright red streaks and her two front teeth were crooked and crossed over at the tips. There was a silver ring in her eyebrow and another in one nostril. She had large brown eyes and looked up at Quinn like a lost puppy. Quinn thought she was a sad little creature.

"Well, why can't you go home?" Quinn asked. "Don't you have a home to go to? Your mother, father?"

"I don't know my dad, he's not around. My mom's boyfriend will just kick me out. He's done it before. I really have no place to go. I stay with Lloyd most of the time."

When she stepped inside the room and into the light, Quinn noticed a large bruise on her left cheek that looked fairly recent.

"What does he do, use you as a punching bag?"

"He can be really nice, sometimes."

"Yeah, I can see that. He looks like a real swell guy. You should find yourself someone with less of a temper."

"This is a small town. There's hardly anyone around here."

"Well there's a highway right down the road. You could get on a bus and get the hell out of this town."

"But I wouldn't know where to go or what to do. I think this is all I've got, right here. I've lived here all my life, this is all I know."

"You're not that dumb, little girl. There is plenty out there. You just have to go look for it. There is a lot more to living than what's in this town."

"But I'm alone and scared."

"We're all alone and scared in this world. But it looks to me like you would be better off alone than with someone like him. At least you could figure out who you are and what you want to do with the rest of your life. You hang around with him too long you're not going to have much of a life. You might not even live long enough to have a life." Quinn was getting all wound up in his own emotion and just babbling on. Who was he to be giving out advice anyway? He knew it was just cheap talk, and she probably could care less about anything this old man had to say. Besides, we're not all alone in this world. He once had Emma, and they'd been together for more than forty-five years. It's just that when it comes down to it, you really only have yourself to take responsibility for your actions. It doesn't really matter. She's going to do what she's going to do.

"Now, look, I'm tired and I'm going to bed. So if you want to spend the night, you can sleep on that sofa over there. I'm too old to be crunched up on that little sofa. There's a blanket on a shelf in the bathroom. I'm going to try and get some sleep now. I've got a long day tomorrow, so you do what you want."

"Oh, gee, thanks. I'll be fine over there. I really appreciate it. I promise I won't bother you any."

Quinn shook his head and crawled back in bed and started to doze off again. Then he heard her voice coming from the sofa across the room. "You can have me if you want." There was a long pause of silence and then he said, "I'll take a rain check."

It was late in the night when he felt Sugar stirring around on the bed. She was always a sound sleeper and normally never moved once they got in bed. Then he heard soft breathing and he caught his breath and had thoughts of Emma, sleeping next to him. A quiet voice said, "The sofa is too short for me, too."

Quinn slowly slid his hand over and touched the warm skin of her body. He started to pull his hand away when she reached out and stopped him. She laid his hand on her naked stomach and placed her hand on top of his. They lay there in silence holding hands, both needing the comfort and warmth of the other, and slept that way all night, hand in hand. It had been a long time since Quinn had felt the warmth of a body next to him. He dreamed sweet dreams of Emma all night long. It was the best sleep he'd had in months.

When Quinn woke the next morning, she was still holding his hand on her stomach, and Sugar was asleep lying between them. He slowly removed his hand and slipped out of bed. It was early and just starting to get light, and he didn't want to disturb her. She looked so innocent lying there in bed next to Sugar and there was no need to wake this poor soul. Jodi was going to need all the rest she could gather up to free herself from her abusive boyfriend and then figure out what to do with her life. Quinn stood staring down at her wondering where this frightened girl would end up.

This isn't my problem, he said to himself, I've my own problems to worry about. He'd already played Mr. Nice Guy by letting her spend the night. So forget about her and get on with your own business, you're not here to save the world.

He left the room and went around to the back of the motel to feed his horse. Bracket heard him coming and whinnied as he approached the stall. "Are you hungry boy?" Asking the obvious and rubbing Bracket's nose. "I hope you slept well; we might have a lot of ground to cover today." Quinn tossed him two flakes and filled the water trough, then sat down on a bale of hay and waited, his elbows on his knees and his chin resting in his hands, watching Bracket chomp away at the hay on the ground.

An hour later he led Bracket around to the front of the motel saddled up and ready to ride. Quinn noticed the motel manager was in his office so he tied Bracket to the post and went inside. The manager greeted him with a good morning and offered him coffee. "There are some doughnuts over on that table. If you'd like one, help yourself."

Quinn told the manager he was leaving this morning but was going to pay him for two more nights. He told him about Jodi, who was in his room, hiding out from her boyfriend. "Just kinda leave her be, okay?" The manager knew who she was and told him he would make sure she was left alone.

"Do you happen have any paper and an envelope I can have?"

"Sure." He reached under the counter and pulled out the motel stationary with Sweet Dreams printed on the letter head and envelope. "Here you go."

"Thanks."

Quinn walked back to his room to get Sugar and the rest of his things. When he walked in, Jodi was still sleeping. Sugar jumped down from the bed as Quinn gathered up his saddlebags and bed role. But before he left, he wrote Jodi a note.

Jodi.
The money is for a bus ticket. You're a nice, pretty girl.
Be good to yourself. The room is yours for two more nights.
The old man and his dog.
P.S. I slept great last night. Thanks.

He put the note and the money in the envelope and set it on the nightstand next to the bed then laid the room key on top of the envelope and somberly moved to the door and quietly opened it, he looked back at Jodi, then locked and pulled it shut.

He had a rush of sadness as he bent over to pick up his dog. He felt confused about all that happened during the night and wanted to put it behind him. Quinn walked over to Bracket who was standing quietly by the post, watching his every move. He set Sugar on the saddle while he tied his saddlebags and bed roll on, then reached in the saddlebag and pulled out the gun that was lying on Emma's ashes and moved it to the other side. He was afraid it might wear a hole in the plastic bag and the ashes would leak out. Before he buckled it, he looked inside. He put his hand in and touched the cold bag. He took a quick breath as he started to choke up and then looked away. He mounted Bracket and sat quietly for a moment with his head down then stared up at the sky, took another deep breath and rode out into the street. He stopped to let a car pass, before turning towards the auto shop.

When he rode up to the shop, he immediately could tell it was a work day. Everything looked completely different now. There were cars and trucks parked everywhere. Two people were standing outside talking and the large bay doors were open with men milling around inside. They were definitely open for business. Quinn got down from his horse, tied him to a tree out in front of the parking lot, sat Sugar on the saddle and walked over to the office. He could hear a loud voice coming from inside. He bent down and peeked through the window and gave a couple quick knocks and opened the door. A man was sitting behind a desk talking on the telephone; he waved Quinn in without looking up, then turned and shouted at someone in the shop.

It had something to do with an employee who was supposed to clean the place up but never showed. "What the hell is going on?" the owner yelled.

"Lloyd got the shit kicked out of him last night." Someone shouted back. "I don't think he's coming in."

"Well, that's just great." He threw up his arms in frustration then turned to Quinn and managed to smile, "What can I do for you?"

Quinn was trying to process all this information he had just heard. Lloyd, works here? He got the shit kicked out of him. This happened last night? Shit...it has to be the same guy.

"Yeah, I've got a big problem. I hope you can help me."

"What's the problem?"

"My truck broke down about six miles outside of town, on the old road. It has a horse trailer with a broken hitch. The jack is so badly bent I can't unhitch the trailer, so I can't drive the truck."

"Man, you do have a problem."

"I know. Can you help me?"

"I'm sure we can fix it. I just don't know when. You can see how busy we are right now."

"Yeah, I can see that." Quinn was getting more and more frustrated at the thought of spending any more time in this withering wasteland of a town. "Can you give some kind of an idea on time?"

"I won't be able to get to it for at least a couple of days."

"No sooner?"

"I'll have to see how the work load goes. If I can get to it sooner, I will."

"Okay, do what you can, here are the keys. I better take your card and I'll check in with you. You won't be able to reach me by phone."

Quinn knew he wasn't going to hang around this little town for two or three days anymore than he would stay on a sinking ship and ride it to the bottom. Hanging around would drive him crazy, and he was already going crazy. He turned to leave and stopped, just before walking out the door he asked, "Say, you wouldn't happen to have a forest service office in town, would you?"

"Yeah, we sure do, it's out at the other end of town. It's an old house and I think it has a sign that says information center or something like that. That's where it is, anyway, you can't miss it.

As Quinn walked back to his horse, he kept thinking about the Lloyd guy who worked in the shop. It's too big of a coincidence not to be the same guy. I hope he's as dumb as he looked, Quinn thought. I sure don't need to tangle with him right now.

Sugar was sleeping on the saddle in the warm sun as he walked up to his horse. Quinn looked up in the sky. There were scattered clouds around, and it looked like there was more rain on the way. He untied Bracket from the tree, lifted Sugar off the saddle, stepped in the stirrup and swung his leg over, took a deep breath, turned Bracket around and headed back towards town. As they rode past the Sweet Dreams Motel, he looked over, hoping Jodi was still asleep in the room. Everything seemed quiet. If he remembered right, young kids can sleep all day if you let them. When he reached the Moose Head Bar he stopped out front and tried to recall what happened. But it was still a foggy blur of bits and pieces he couldn't quite put together. The bar was closed, but standing at the door were three old guys talking, waiting for it to open. Quinn gave a little nod and pressed on. He felt like joining them. What better way to pass the day, after day, after day, than spending it in a bar drinking with some old farts like himself?

He rode the last eight or nine blocks thinking how tired and old the town looked. It was no different than I am, he thought, we've outlived our better days. On almost every street there seemed to be a deserted rundown house and he could feel the deep distress the town was going through. There was no one here to pick it up and dust it off and make it bright and shiny again. There was no reason to—when it's over, it's over.

Quinn spotted the house. It was a small, single-story wood structure with a raised porch that stretched across the entire front. Over the entrance hung a sign that read, "Information Center." He rode up to investigate. A brick walkway led up to the entrance with tall trees lining the parking lot on the south side of the house. The grass in the front yard was just now starting to turn green. There was no indication of a forest service office.

Quinn sat on his horse and stared at the house. It looked deserted, except for one car in the parking lot. He stepped down from the saddle and walked Bracket up to the house and tied him to a porch post. He put Sugar back on the saddle and walked up the steps to the front door. The door was unlocked, so he took off his hat and went inside. It was a large room with a long counter that divided the room in half. Behind the counter were two desks each with a few papers and a telephone. Against the opposite wall were four metal folding chairs.

"Hello, anyone home?" Quinn leaned over the counter and glanced up the hallway. "Hello… anyone?"

"I'll be right with you." A voice came from somewhere in the back of the house. A few minutes later a man appeared down the hallway, shifting his pants up in back as he walked towards him. "What can I do for you?" He was a tall, slender, middle-aged man in full ranger garb.

"Well, I was wondering if you could help me out with some directions."

"Sure, it's a small town, everything is pretty easy to find around here. What are you looking for?"

"No, it's nothing in town. I have a cabin back in the Bear Creek area. I'm going to ride up there on horseback, and it'd sure help me if I had a trail map."

"On horseback…why would you want to ride there on a horse?" The ranger asked, sounding a little concerned while scratching his chin and looking Quinn up and down.

"Well, it's a long story. My truck broke down along with my horse trailer and I'm trying to get back up to my cabin. Anyway, I was hoping you had some trail maps of the area. It'd sure make the trip a lot easier if you did."

"You sound a little crazy to me. Are you just trying to get in a mess of trouble?"

"Not at all. I'm pretty sure about this."

"That would be one hell of a ride even if you knew the way."

Quinn didn't say anything. The ranger just stood there with his hands on his hips, looking at Quinn, not sure what to make of him.

The ranger finally said, "Well, just for my own curiosity, come on in the back and I'll show you what I have. There's this large wall map of the area, and I'm sure we can find Bear Creek on it. Most of the trails are logging trails, but there are some hiking and riding trails through some parts of the mountains. We'll just see what we can put together for you."

Quinn walked around the counter and followed the ranger into a room that had maps lying around everywhere. When he saw the large map on the wall, the first thing he recognized was his destination. There it was, the little lake above the river. There were other lakes on the map, but he knew that was the one. It didn't look that far away, on the map. I can make that ride he said to himself, I know I can. I just need a little help finding the right trails.

It took a lot of back-tracking and dead ends, but after a while, between the two of them they figured out the easiest way up there. Quinn drew it all out on a piece of paper, with as many landmarks as the ranger knew about. Some of it was very iffy. Quinn had ridden in the mountains long enough to know the pitfalls of a hand-written trail map. He also knew how to make his own trail if he had to but the map should keep him from getting lost.

The ranger stood back a few feet to check Quinn out again. "I don't want you to get me wrong, but you know I'm not in favor of you doing this. I don't know how old you are or what kind of physical shape you're in, but to me, you look a little over the hill to be trying this by yourself. Even if everything goes right and you don't run into any problems along the way, it's still going to take you, maybe, two or three days of hard riding. Or hell, it could even take you longer."

Quinn put his hat on and smiled. "Then I better get going."

"There is still snow up there and the trails aren't in great shape. I hear it might even snow tonight."

"I know you don't think it's a good idea for me to be doing this, and I appreciate your concern for my safety. As hard as it is for you to understand what I'm doing, it's just as hard for me to explain it to you. But believe me, it's just something I have to do. Anyway, I've been riding in these mountains all of my life. I just haven't been over on this side before." Quinn was trying to convince the guy he would be okay, so he wouldn't ask any more questions and get on his way.

"I have nothing but time," Quinn finally said.

"You're making a big mistake." The ranger's voice sounded like a warning. "Does anyone know you're taking this trip?"

"Yeah, you do."

"Would you do me a favor?"

"Sure."

"Here's my card, when and if you somehow make it, will you give me a call? I'd just like to know you made it alright."

"Sure, I can do that, Thanks for caring"

"I don't want to have to send up a crew looking for your body in a few weeks."

"Now you're just trying to build my confidence." Quinn chuckled.

"What I'd really like to do is change your mind."

"No can do, it's done. I'll give you a call first thing, I promise." He looked at the ranger's card. "Bill, is it?"

"Yeah, that's right, Bill Patrick."

Quinn thanked the man again for his help and walked outside. He mounted his horse, secured Sugar, turned Bracket around and started to ride off.

"Wait!"

He turned back to see Bill standing on the porch.

"Is that your dog?"

"Yeah."

"Are you taking her with you?"

"Well, I was thinking I might leave her but…"

"Why don't you leave her with me and pick her up on your way back? It would be a lot easier for you and your dog."

"That's real nice of you to offer, but I think we're all three in this together now, and I wouldn't want to break up a threesome." He turned Bracket around again and started to ride away.

"There's still a lot of snow up there," Bill yelled.

Quinn didn't turn, he just held up a hand in acknowledgment, then slowly headed out of town.

# CHAPTER SIX

A cold wind blew down from the mountain and swirled around them stirring up dust along with a scattering of rain drops. Quinn rode leisurely along the shoulder between the blacktop and a muddy drainage ditch. The day had started out warm and sunny, but now the deep blue sky was gradually being overtaken by dark, ominous clouds, and it looked like more rain was on the way. They came to a large fenced in pasture where a half dozen horses gathered together with their heads down, engrossed in the new spring grass. Two of the horses wandered over to the fence line to investigate the oncoming horse and rider. Quinn glanced up as they approached then turned back, dropping his head, lost in half sleep and continued on.

There was little traffic on the road. A pick-up had passed by earlier, heading into town, and a car towing a boat trailer went by a few minutes later. Quinn could hear a car approaching from behind. He didn't turn around, even though it was the first car to come his way. He just kept on riding with his head down as it drew near.

The car slowed and pulled alongside of him. Quinn glanced over at the darken windows and saw two people sitting in the front seat. The passenger slowly rolled his window down, and Quinn leaned forward to see who it was.

"Tithead… is that you?"

"Fuck you! My name ain't Tithead, asshole."

Quinn was fully alert now. "Well, that's what your friend was calling you last night." And he smiled back.

"Oh, yeah, well, you should really be scared at what he's going to do to you."

"Scared like you are, you mean?" The jousting of words invigorated Quinn as he straightened up in the saddle.

"I'm not scared of him."

"Oh, then why do you let him call you Tithead?"

"Fuck you, old man. You're going to get yours. Let's get out of here." Quinn heard the driver laugh and remark…"Shit man, he gotcha on that one."

"Shut up and drive."

Quinn could tell Tithead was boiling inside. They turned the car around in the middle of the street and peeled out, heading back toward town. Quinn watched as they sped away, hoping that was the end of it. But he knew they were not going to let that brief conversation end the way it did, they were going to get at him one way or another.

Quinn rode on, glancing back over his shoulder every once in a while. He didn't want to be caught off guard. And sure enough, a few minutes later he saw them turn onto the main road and head in his direction.

As the car crept closer, Quinn reached back behind him into his saddlebag and without turning around he slid his gun out and held it against his right leg, out of sight and next to Sugar. His fingers were stiff and still hurting from the pool stick incident as he cocked the hammer back. He could hear the tires on the loose gravel as they came closer. His horse had never been gun-broke, and he wasn't sure how he was going to handle what was about to happen. Quinn leaned forward and whispered in Bracket's ear. "You're not going to like the sound of this. I hope you don't freak out on me. Sorry, boy."

When the car came up next to him, Tithead leaned out of the window, the wind whipping his hair across his face, his hands gripping tight to a baseball bat. He took a mighty swing. Quinn could see Tithead's shadow on the ground and was ready. He ducked under just as the bat flew past his head, clipping off his hat and skimming the back of his head. When Tithead missed his mark with his hard swing, his momentum spun him around, the bat sliding from his hand, cracking the windshield. Bracket jiggered to the side as Quinn raised the gun from his leg and aimed at the passing back tire and squeezed the trigger. The gun quivered in his hand as a slug exploded from the barrel, piercing the tire. At the sound of the gun going off and the tire blowing out, Bracket leaped straight up in the air, then jumped across the drainage ditch next to the fence-line.

The driver stepped on the gas and cut the wheel sharply. The car spun around and the rear end slid down into the drainage ditch, its rear wheels became submerged in mud up to the axles. The car sat motionless; its head lights pointing to the heavens.

Quinn got Bracket under control, then searched the grass for his gun, which he'd dropped during the mayhem. He found it, glinting in the tall grass and picked it up along with his hat then walked up to the car. "You boys alright in there?" he asked.

"Go fuck yourself!" Tithead snapped.

"I think I cut my head," the young driver said. "Can you see any blood? It hurts."

"Shut up, you little prick."

"You know Tithead, or whatever your name is, no good can come from hanging around with this loser Lloyd, and when he goes down, as he will, he's going to take you down with him. It's just something to think about. Well, anyway, you know he's going to be a little pissed-off at you two, so you better get your story straight. But I'll tell you what... if I see any help up the road, I'll send them back for you."

Quinn mounted up and rode on and never looked back. All he had on his mind now was the job that lay before him. He would keep the promise he'd made to Emma no matter what. He was so tired of dealing with people. All he wanted was to be left alone. It felt good to be leaving that tired old town behind him, but with all the stillness around him, he began to worry that his thoughts would let the sadness build back up inside, the sadness that really never went away but was hanging around on the fringe of his mind.

He had barley ridden four miles when he could feel it in the pit of his stomach. He was just staring again, off into the distance at nothing. The grieving hurt had returned, and all he could do was think about how much he missed his wife, and if it was really worth going on without her.

He wanted to get off his horse and lie on the side of the road, shut his eyes and let it all be over. What the hell was he doing, anyway? There was no way he would go back to that town and wait three or four days in that crummy little motel room. So he kept moving and the more he moved the more things became clearer. He still had the chore to do and then it might all come to an end. That had always been an option.

As he rode on up the road, the day seemed to drag on and on and he hadn't even started into the mountains. He felt so tired, and he was cold and his body ached, and he tried to put it out of his mind. He started to think of Emma and how she had felt during all those months of grieving after her father passed away. He remembered that time so well. He'd never forget it.

It was 1978. Emma's father had suffered from congestive heart failure and was on oxygen twenty-four hours a day. No longer able to travel up in the mountain's high altitude, he grew depressed, knowing he'd never see his cabin again, the one place he loved most in the world.

Emma never missed a chance to see her father. She went by to visit almost every day. He'd always put on an act for her, as if everything was fine and he was doing better and soon would be able to make it up to the cabin. He'd plan trips with her and talk about the rides they'd go on. She knew he'd never get better but always thought perhaps he had another year of life. She expected to have more time to say her goodbyes.

Then came that night when she arrived home, after her visit with her dad, tired and sad, and decided a hot bath would help. While she was soaking in the tub, the phone in the bedroom rang. Quinn picked up the receiver and heard the voice on the phone that would change their lives for years.

"Who was that on the phone?" Emma asked from the bathtub. Quinn walked up to the bathroom door, stopped and then slowly opened it. He stood there in the doorway with his head down, trying to think of what to say.

"Is Dad alright?" Emma asked, sensing something was wrong.

"That was the hospital. Your father just passed away." As the words were coming off his lips, a sound like he had never heard before echoed around them. It was so loud that it rattled the mirror on the wall and moved items on the counter and the sound seemed to linger throughout the house. It sounded like it came from the depth of her soul. Emma leaped from the tub screaming, water splashing out of the tub and dripping from her body as she ran hysterically through the house.

He grabbed her robe and went after her. When he caught up to her, he pulled her down on the sofa and held her. She was fighting him and yelling and wanting to run. She wanted to run as far from the hurt and pain as she could. Quinn didn't know what to do. He just sat on her, trying to calm her and hold her still. He held her face in his hands talking softly to her, telling her over and over how much he loved her and that everything was going to be fine. She looked at him, with her eyes opened wide but never seeing him. She just stared off into space. It seemed like hours went by before he finally was able to pick her up and put her in bed. She slept all night. In the morning she was quiet and wouldn't talk. Her mother came over and sat with her. Quinn called their two daughters, who were away at school and told them what had happened.

Emma went into a heartbreaking depression. The worst of her depression lasted for more than a year. There were days when she'd never leave her bed. Everyone in the family was worried that Emma was dying, dying of a broken heart. Emma thought living seemed hopeless. Everyone in the family, in some way, was affected. Together and individually they tried to encourage her to get out of bed, to get dressed, to go outside into the sunlight, maybe, to take a ride in the car, to do something, to do anything but nothing seemed to work.

The days and the weeks went by slowly. Each day seemed like the last. She'd get up, walk through the house and sometimes say a few words that made you think things were back to normal. But nothing changed. She just went back to her room, got into bed and stayed there the rest of the day. This went on for over a year and a half, until their daughter Jessica finally came to her and said, "Look, you can't keep doing this. It's not fair to us. I need you. Dad needs you. We all need you. You've got to get up and get over this, whatever it is you're doing. You've grieved long enough."

Emma understood all that Jesse said and knew she was right and also knew she had to pull her life back together. Sadly, Emma agreed that she was being selfish and admitted that it wasn't fair to her children or Quinn. She began to make a real effort to return to daily life, but the sadness in her heart was still there and wouldn't go away.

In the spring of the second year, as the season started to warm and the days grew longer Emma's spirit started to feel a new birth of life. Early one morning, Emma came to Quinn and said, "I want to go open Dad's cabin."

He looked at her in amazement. Just yesterday she had little desire to even go outside, and now she wanted to go to the cabin. "Are you sure?" He said.

"Yes, I've been thinking about it. Dad would want us to use the cabin, and I feel close to him up there. You know, the two of us would sometimes open it together."

"Yes, I know, but are you sure that's what you want to do. There's a lot of work to do when we first open the cabin."

"I know that! I've done it plenty of times." Emma said, with salty determination.

Quinn wasn't so sure about this idea, but it couldn't hurt to get her out of the house and away from the ranch. "Okay, let's go." he said hoping this might be a real breakthrough.

They began gathering the things they needed for the trip. Quinn called his brother Will to let him know what they were going to do. Will thought it sounded like a great idea. He told Quinn not to worry and to take as much time as they needed. He and his boys could handle things at the ranch till they got back.

Emma called and told her mother about their trip. "I won't be gone long. There are things I have to do and I don't want you to worry about me. I'll be fine." Her mother said she felt good about their going. The family always had so much fun when they were there, and this could only help put her life back on track.

In the morning Quinn loaded their horses in the trailer, while Emma helped pack up the truck. She was almost smiling when they took off for the cabin, but there was little conversation during the drive. They both sat quietly, listening to the sound of the tires, its humming lulling them each into private thoughts. He didn't ask any questions about the sudden change in her demeanor, or the real reason why she wanted to go to the cabin. He knew he wouldn't get much of an answer anyway.

When they arrived at the cabin, Quinn stopped the truck and jumped out to check the horses. Emma just sat in the cab and stared out the windshield at the front of the cabin while thoughts of her father surged through her mind. This was going to be harder than she thought.

Quinn walked around the truck to open her door for her. "Give me a minute," she said.

"Take your time. I'll go unload the horses and start up the well, see if we have any leaks." He smiled and touched her on her shoulder, then turned and walked away, leaving her with her memories. Quinn had become used to her like this. He knew he had to give her as much space as she needed.

By the time he was through fixing a leak under the cabin. Emma had already cleaned away spider webs and dusted, made up the bed and put the food away, and was starting to prepare dinner for later that evening.

Quinn walked in and looked around. "The place looks pretty good, doesn't it?"

"There were a lot of spider webs and mice droppings, but it's shaping up. Dinner will be ready in about an hour," she told him, not looking up from her preparations. "Fix yourself a drink. I'll call you when it's ready."

Quinn was really pleased with the way things were going. She had surprised him with all she had accomplished. There was always a lot of work to do that first day, and she'd jumped right in without hesitation.

For the first two days at the cabin, everything went along smoothly.

Emma was up every morning rain or shine and had plenty of things to keep herself busy. There was no more lying in bed all day grieving. She seemed to Quinn almost like her old self, always finding things that needed tending to. But there was something different that he couldn't quite put his finger on. She seemed to be keeping her distance. She went on a short trail ride, by herself. Their conversations were pleasant but never long.

It was early in the morning on the third day when she told Quinn, "I'm going to take Dad's ashes up in the mountains today."

"You brought your dad's ashes?"

Emma didn't answer, she just nodded her head.

"That's a long ride. Are you sure you're ready for that?"

"Yes, I've been there before, I know what to expect."

"Okay, I'll go with you. I'll get the horses saddled up."

"No!" She said emphatically. "I don't want you to go. I have to do this alone."

He thought she must view this as part of the healing process. "I don't think that's a good idea. That's a rough ride this time of year. What if you get in trouble?" He was becoming uneasy because he knew he couldn't stop her, once she made up her mind.

"I can do it. This is something I have to do."

"The river can run high and fast this time of year and…"

"I know I can do it." She interrupted. "Please, don't do this to me. I want to be by myself. I'll be okay, I promise." That was final.

"Alright, I'll tell you what. If you're not back by one, I'm going to come up after you." She knew he was upset with her, but she didn't care. She glared at him for a moment, then turned and walked out to get her horse ready.

The hours passed slowly and Quinn was getting frustrated. His horse was saddled and ready to go. It was only twelve fifteen, early, but still, there was no sign of her. He couldn't stand it any longer. He was going nuts and waiting around was not one of his best attributes. Quinn mounted his horse and started off after her. It was a good two-hour ride to the river crossing, and another fifteen minutes up to the meadow where the creek started.

As he rode the last few hundred yards and past the large boulder, everything was looking normal. Emma's horse was grazing quietly on the tall grass in the meadow. Emma was sitting on the rocks by the bubbling stream, holding an empty bag. The ashes had been sent on their way.

He called out to her and she turned and smiled at him. "I rode up across the face of the canyon." Her voice trailed off. "I thought he would have liked that." Her smile was beaming. She looked so happy. "I'm ready to go home now."

It was as if all the heartrending months had been waiting for just this one moment. His eyes filled with tears as he welcomed her beautiful smile. It was good to have her back.

Quinn could now relate to the way she had spent months alone in her room and days sitting on her bed leafing through old photo albums; how she preferred to be alone and remained isolated for days at a time. At the time Quinn had thought it was strange, but now he understood.

Maybe, it hasn't been long enough, he thought, but he wasn't sure how long it was supposed to last. Is there a time limit for missing someone? Should he just sit down and wait for the time to pass, until it dissipates? The one thing he knew for sure, it wasn't going anywhere. Emma had improved after fulfilling her promise to her father. Is that the answer, the ashes and fulfilling the promise?

Quinn turned his horse onto the first dirt crossroad. There were open fields on both sides, fenced in by barbed wire. He rode alongside the fields until he came to the next intersection, then turned onto another dirt road. He continued along the fence line for about a mile, then stopped and looked around at his surroundings. Something didn't look right. He reached into his shirt pocket and took out the map he'd made at the ranger station. He held it up and studied his drawing. He knew he had already made his first mistake. How was he ever going get through the mountains if he couldn't even get past this first, easiest step? He looked around again. He needed to be on the other side of this field, beyond those trees.

Turning, he looked behind him and thought I'm going to have to ride all the way back and around this field... Or maybe I can cut across it. He rode up a little further until he spotted a fence posts that had fallen over where portions of the wire were lying on the ground. If he could get his horse over that wire and safely on the other side of the fence, they could cut across the field and save all that time back tracking.

Quinn dismounted, dropped the reins and set Sugar on the ground, then walked over to the fallen fence post. Grass had grown over the wires, making them difficult to find. He grabbed hold of the post and pulled it up straight in order to expose the hidden wires, then dropped it back on the ground. Taking hold of Bracket's bridle, he helped him cross over the wire into the open field. He had to stand on some of the higher wires and press them down with his boot. Sugar scurried across after them and sat, waiting to be lifted back onto the saddle. After his horse made it safely through the barbed wire, he said smiling with pride. "Well, that wasn't so bad, and it's going to save us some time, too." He thought things would go a lot smoother now that they were out of that crazy town.

Quinn went back and straightened up the fence post. This time he wound the loose wire around the top of the post to keep it upright. As he was finishing up with the fence, Sugar started barking. It sounded like a warning. He looked up and saw a pickup truck hauling ass down the dirt road in their direction, a cloud of dust following behind. "Oh, shit, what the hell is this?" Just when everything was going so smooth, he saw nothing but trouble coming. He turned and walked over to his horse, grabbed the reins, his dog and climbed into the saddle, just as the truck came to a screeching stop. As the dust from the truck settled over them, he waved his arm at the cloud and could see an old man and woman sitting inside.

The man bolted out of the cab and yelled over the bed of the truck. "What the hell do you think you're doing? Get the hell off my property! Now!" He was a man about Quinn's age, short, with a big belly, wearing bib overalls and a beat-up straw hat. His red face was full of wrinkles and a two-week old white beard.

Quinn turned his horse around to look at the man. "I'm just taking a short cut across this unplanted field," he said, stressing the word 'unplanted.' "No harm meant."

"You're not going anywhere. Get your ass back over here," he shouted.

"Now, that's no way for you to act, after I fixed your downed fence for you."

"You're on my property and you're not going anywhere, damn it."

Quinn sat on his horse and looked at the old man for a few moments, then shook his head in disgust and, without saying another word, turned his horse and started walking across the field towards the trees.

"You son of a bitch!" The man reached inside the cab of the truck and quickly grabbed his rifle off the rear window rack. His wife started yelling, "Frank, put that goddamn gun back. Don't be stupid."

When Quinn heard the word 'gun', he gave Bracket a kick and put him into a slow lope. He could hear them fighting and yelling at each other behind him but didn't stop to listen to what they were saying. Then he heard the gun go off. "Oh my God, the idiot is shooting at us." Quinn gave Bracket a hard kick and pushed him into a full on run. They headed for a gully right before the grove of trees. He held Sugar securely in his arms. She'd never been on a running horse before and he didn't want to drop her. He could tell she was frightened, not of the gunfire, but from the sudden burst of speed.

Quinn figured they would be safe and out of danger if he could just make it to the gully. He heard another bullet spinning past his head just as they reached the top of the small ravine. He rode along the edge looking for a way to safety. It wasn't very deep, and the banks were on a slight angle, so he turned Bracket down into the bottom where they were out of sight of the old rifleman.

Quinn stopped, jumped off his horse and crawled up the bank to the top, taking Sugar with him. He wanted to see what they were going to do next. They were standing next to the truck quarreling and shouting at each other. The woman had grabbed hold of his riffle with one hand and was slapping him on his head with the other. They seemed so busy fighting among themselves that Quinn figured they'd forget all about him.

He rolled over onto his back. He was exhausted and needed a breather. He took his hat off and set it on the ground next to him and let loose of Sugar so she could run around and stretch her legs. He reached inside his coat pocket and pulled out a cigar, lit it and took a deep drag, letting the smoke slowly rise from his mouth. He lay there enjoying his smoke, looking back over his shoulder every now and then to see what the old man and woman were doing. They finally got in their truck and drove away. He was beginning to relax a little, but it was now starting to rain again, not a lot, just enough to keep the dust down. He was enjoying the cigar and his short moment of quiet time, but he knew it had to end.

He forced himself up and slid down the embankment. He walked back to his horse, picked up Sugar, took the reins in hand and walked Bracket about fifty yards up the gully before mounting him. He rode up the slope and into the trees.

It took him about ten minutes to work his way through thick growth. As he came out of the heavily wooded trees, there was a ten-foot dirt embankment that they had to climb in order to reach the road. It was dirt and rocks that were bladed off to the side when they made the road. Quinn rode up on an angle to the top of the embankment, and when he reached the road, he stopped and checked the map to make sure it was the right road this time. His mistake with the wrong road had almost cost him his life. If he were going to die on this journey, he wanted to do it on his own terms, not by the hands of some crazy old farmer or two young kids who couldn't even wipe their own ass. The map checked out, it was the road he wanted. About 300 yards up ahead, as indicated on his map, he found the trail head.

The trail head was an old logging road that wound around into the mountains. On his map, it showed there was a sign about five miles up ahead that indicated where the trails started. There he should find a smaller hiking trail that would lead them into the forest and through the mountains to his destination. He had no idea what the trail was going to be like. In all his riding in these mountains, he'd never been on this side before, but he knew that no matter where you were in the mountains, these small hiking trails are all similar. There were good parts and bad parts to them. He also knew his horse—he knew that Bracket could make it through just about anything. He wasn't going to let the condition of the trails worry him. It was the ache in his heart and the yearning to be with Emma that troubled him. Being alone in a lonely place in the middle of nowhere he could handle, but how was he going to continue to deal with that yearning?

Storm clouds were building up over his left shoulder to the northwest, forming a thick gray background for the broad plains below and the higher hills beyond. It was still early in the day, but it was getting dark. They turned onto the logging road and started up into the mountain. It was full of twists and turns as they climbed higher and higher. When he rounded a sharp bend in the road, Quinn heard a rumbling sound that began to get louder and then became a roar. He looked up just in time to see a huge logging truck with a full load barreling around the bend. He just had time to get Bracket off to the side as the truck went screaming past, spraying them with dust and gravel. And he'd thought the farmer was his biggest threat.

He got Bracket back on the road and tried to shake as much of the dust off as he could before going any farther. The higher they went, the more snow they were beginning to see, mostly along the sides of the road or under trees.

When they finally reached the turn off to the small hiking trail, the weather was turning colder, and he knew if it started raining, it would turn to snow as night drew near and the temperature fell. He hadn't planned this trip around snow. He hadn't planned anything, and he sure as hell wasn't prepared for snow. It was getting colder.

From time to time he would look down at Sugar. She was shivering and would stare back at him with eyes that asked, are we almost there? "I'm sorry girl. I should have left you back there in town. I didn't know it was going to be like this."

# CHAPTER SEVEN

A cold chill ran down Quinn's spine. He had just realized that all this time, he'd never called his daughter to let her know where he was, what had happened or what he was doing. Although he couldn't really tell her what he was doing, because she'd freak out. She'd never be able to handle it. He knew they must be worried sick that he hadn't called after he'd promised he would. But there was nothing he could do about it; it was just one more thing to stress about. He'd left his cell phone in the truck, but it wouldn't have done him any good, not up in the mountains. He wouldn't be able to contact her until he got to the cabin, and he had no idea how long that might take.

They're just going to have to wait it out, sort of like he and Emma had done when Anna was in junior high school. She had gone to the movies with a girlfriend, and when the show let out she called the house to tell her mother she'd be home in twenty minutes. Her friend's father was picking them up after the movie let out. While they were waiting for their ride, this good-looking high school boy started up a conversation with the two girls out in front of the theater and offered to give her a ride home. This was really exciting. He was one of the most popular boys in town. How could she say no to him? So Anna got in the car with the young boy and left her friend, begrudgingly, to ride home with her dad. The boy asked Anna if she'd mind if he stopped off at a friend's house for a minute before he took her home. She said that's fine. Maybe she'd get a chance to meet more of the in crowd.

But it didn't work out that way. She was left standing inside the front door alone as the boy went off with his friends. It was a small group of high school kids sitting around, drinking beer and smoking cigarettes. Some of the boys were watching a game on television. No one paid any attention to her. Anna stood by the door, her hands clasped together in front of her, feeling alone and scared and not knowing what to do. A girl finally came to the door to leave. She smiled at Anna, then opened the door and stepped outside shutting the door behind her. A moment later the door opened again and the girl stood there looking at Anna. "How old are you?"

"Thirteen."

"What's your name?"

"Anna Adams."

"What are you doing here?"

"That boy, the one with long black hair, he said he'd drive me home from the movies. He said he'd just stop here for a minute. That was over an hour ago."

"Where do you live?"

"Out north, on the county road."

"You live out in the country?"

Anna nodded her head.

"Do you have any money?"

"I have a dollar left."

"Give it to me. I'll need it for gas."

The girl brought Anna safely home. Quinn couldn't remember her name, but he was sure Anna would never forget her or that night. Anna had worried her parents to death. Now, he was doing the same thing to her. He knew what she was going through, and all he could do was say he was sorry.

He rode the rest of the morning and into the afternoon through tall pines, keeping to the narrow trail on the side of the ridge. When he rounded his first real sharp bend on the trail, the large lava bed appeared in front of him, the one he had marked on his map. If nothing else, Quinn knew he was on the right trail, and that alone made him feel a little better. A cold gust of wind hit him as he circled the lava bed and found himself on a rim rock, overlooking the vast sweep of the country to the south and east. He stopped and sat his horse for a moment to gaze upon the land below. Even in the rain, the land had a special beauty to it, the dark blue pointed pines rising up out of the black forest. Off in the distance, he could see a curtain of rain sweep across the land, changing shades of blues as it passed in front of him. Quinn reached down and scratched Sugar's chin, then turned his horse and started back into the mountain where the trail began to narrow even more and grew thick with trees. The wind started to pick up, blowing along the trail through the trees, and they were riding straight into it.

As the wind blew at them, Quinn held his head down to keep from losing his hat and protect his face from the cold. He kept thinking he was hearing the whispering again. No, he thought, it's just the wind in the trees. He really wasn't sure anymore. He could almost make out the words this time, but he didn't understand them. Not just the words, but why. Only crazy people hear voices. "Am I going crazy? Sometimes I think I am crazy. So hearing voices in the wind shouldn't surprise me. It's all so weird." Quinn was talking to himself out loud, over the blowing wind, something else crazy people did.

It was getting colder. He stopped and swung his leg up over Bracket's back and stepped out of the saddle, then walked away with his back to his horse and dog. "Isn't this stupid?" he thought. I'm out here in the middle of nowhere, turning my back on a horse and dog just to pee. He looked back over his shoulder and smiled, Bracket and Sugar were also peeing, the three of them all at the same time—now that's bonding.

He untied his slicker from the saddle and put it on over his coat. It was getting so cold it would probably soon be turning to snow.

When he got back on his horse, he put Sugar in her sling and his coat around her, to help protect her from the cold. They started off again, continuing up into the mountains.

About two hours later the snow came. Big large snowflakes began floating down around them. The wind had stopped, but now it was snowing and he could tell it wasn't going to let up. This snow he could handle for a while but Quinn was thinking maybe he should stop before it got worse. He needed to find shelter and wood for a fire, then wait it out until morning.

The snow kept falling, but the trail began to flatten out, and he could see what looked like a small meadow just ahead. When they reached the top of the rise, the land opened up into a spacious field of winter grass surrounded by trees and patches of snow. At one end of the meadow was a grouping of large boulders that might work as shelter against the wind and cold. There were lots of fallen branches around that would make for good firewood. It seemed like as good a place to stop as he was likely to find. He hoped that it would give them some protection from the real storm that was sure to hit them later that night.

They rode into the meadow and crossed a small stream on the way over to the large boulders. Quinn stopped and slid off his horse to the ground. He set Sugar down and she immediately started running here and there, smelling everything around her, loving her freedom. He unsaddled Bracket and placed his saddle and bedroll up against the boulders, as far out of the weather as he could, then walked Bracket back to the small stream to drink.

As he was standing there holding Bracket's lead line, he noticed fish swimming in a shallow pool around the roots of a large tree growing at edge of the stream. He let go of the lead line and walked across the stream to the other side. He quietly lay down on his stomach and pushed up his sleeve and slid his arm into the ice-cold water. At first it felt good on his sore fingers, but then they began to ache. He lay there staying perfectly still, not moving a muscle as the fish swam over and around his hand. He waited for just the right moment, then, in a blink of an eye, flipped a nice-size trout onto the bank.

When he was a young boy, he use to try flipping fish with his dad but never had the patience for any success. Things are different when you get older and haven't eaten in almost two days. After cleaning the fish, he took Bracket back to the boulders where they would camp for the night.

He put the hobbles on Bracket so he couldn't wander too far. Then he began gathering enough wood to make it through the night. He built a fire and set a thin flat rock in the center of the flames to cook his fish on. He had never tried this before. He never had to. In a normal situation he would have all his camping equipment, and there was nothing normal about this trip, but it actually worked out quite well. The fish was a little rare in places, so he picked at it with his knife and fingers. It was better than nothing, he told himself. He had dog food for the dog and meadow grass for his horse. Life was good.

Quinn stacked the firewood next to where he was going to sleep. Getting up and down all night to stoke the fire would be too hard on him. With a large pile of wood next to him, he could reach over grab a dead branch, toss it on the fire without even getting up, then go back to sleep. That was his plan, anyway.

He took Sugar and put her next to him under his blanket. Then he stretched out and got as comfortable as he could and stared at the fire. He lay still, gazing at the fire and watching the flames and the hot red ash as they drifted up into the stars. The fire slowly began to get larger and the flames climbed high and higher into the dark sky, and suddenly he was back in that terrible night years ago when fire had nearly cost him and Emma their lives.

They'd been dating for about six months, and they were on their way home from a concert in the city. It was around eleven o'clock at night, there was a lot of traffic on the road and it had been raining all evening. They came around a bend in the highway, and there was a stalled car in their lane next to the center divider. Quinn tried to change lanes and go around, but in the heavy rain, the lights from the oncoming cars made it hard to judge their speed and distance. The cars were all going way too fast for the road conditions and he couldn't change lanes safely.

He slowed and finally came to a stop behind the stalled car, then looked in his rear view mirror and saw that the car directly behind them was going too fast and was not going to stop.

"We're going to get hit!" Quinn yelled. "Brace yourself!" The car hit them so hard, that the front of their car went up in the air and landed on the back of the car in front of them.

The car began to fill with smoke. Quinn glanced back and witnessed the first flame as it leaped into view. The back seat was on fire and soon the entire car was surrounded by the flames. He could see people outside Emma's window trying to get close to the car to free them but the flames were so intense they couldn't get near the doors; they tried holding up clothing to protect themselves, but the flames kept pushing them back.

"Try rolling down your window," Quinn shouted.

"I can't, it's broken. The handle just keeps spinning around." Emma said, her voice shaking with fear.

"Mine is too, the doors are jammed. I can't get it opened." They put their backs against each other and started kicking the doors with all their might. The doors did not open. Emma lifted up her bare feet and slammed them against her window. Once, twice, and on the third kick, her window shattered into a million tiny pieces of sparkling light, all in different colors, their sharp edges reflecting off the fire. You could see every tiny sparkle as they floated up through the flames spreading out and moving slowly until they were gone.

"Jump!" Quinn yelled.

"No, I can't. I'm scared."

Now the fire was coming in through the broken out window. Quinn grabbed Emma, turned her around to face the open window, then putting his hand under her butt, pushed her through the fire. The people standing outside took hold of her and pulled her through the burning flames.

"Roll her on the ground!" someone shouted. "Her clothes are on fire." They threw Emma down on the rain-soaked pavement and started patting out the fire on her clothes. Other spectators grabbed Quinn and helped pull him through the window. As they rolled him on the ground, he looked around trying to find Emma.

When Quinn got to his feet he started to run, then turned and ran the other way. He stopped and yelled out her name. "Where are you, Emma?" He couldn't see her anywhere. Then there was a loud explosion. He turned around and saw their car had blown up and was completely engulfed in flames. The flames were 20 to 30 feet above the overpass. He jumped back from the heat and started running again to find Emma. Then he saw her, sitting up high on the embankment in the wet ivy on the side of the highway. She was rolled up like a ball, with her arms around her knees and her head buried in her arms. He could see her quivering in the dark with the rain falling. He raced up to her, sat down beside her and put his arms around her. He held her tight and kissed her on her cheek.

"Honey, are you okay?" He asked.

"I don't know." She was crying. "I've never been so scared in my whole life. I thought we were going to die, I thought we were going to die." She kept repeating, "I was so scared." over and over in a mumbling voice. She finally looked up at him, still crying. He could see the reflection of the burning car in her moist eyes. She turned to him and held his face in her hands. "Look at me!" she said, "Why is God doing this to me? Does God want me dead?" Emma began to cry harder.

"It was an accident, things happen. I think God has plans for you and that's why he spared your life," Quinn had no idea why she felt God wanted her dead. "You just saved our lives, Emma. I don't know how you did it. A second longer and it would have been too late. It was truly a miracle. So God must have plans for you. He wants you to live." They sat holding each other in their arms. It was as if the fire had fused their souls together that night. They were married four months later.

The fire that had sparked that memory was dying down, and he felt a chill that brought him out of his trance. He was shaking, not from the cold, but from the memories of that night and one of the most special moments of his life.

He reached over and threw another log on the fire, small, hot embers flying into the air as the log landed on the smoldering ash. He had tears in his eyes. That accident had happened over forty years ago, and it came back in his memory as though it had just happened. Quinn even remembered the song they had heard the night before on the radio. It was the first time either of them had heard it. They liked it so much they decided to make it their song. It all seems so ironic now, as he thought back to the two of them sitting on the side of the road, watching the shell of their car smoldering in the rain while the fire died down. "Come on, baby, light my fire."

Quinn always thought he would be the first to go. He assumed the wife outlives her husband. "Why her, I was four years older. I should have been the one to go first, not Emma." This was always so confusing to him. Why one person and not the other? How does God decide on who lives and who dies? He'd joke with Emma sometimes, telling her that he was going to live longer than her because of her smoking.

"Oh, so after I die you can go find yourself some nice young twenty-year-old to replace me?' Emma would ask. Then Quinn would laugh, "Yeah that sounds like a great idea, that's what I'll do." Then Emma would get serious and say, "You'll be sorry if you do live longer than me."

Now, after all those years, he realized what she had meant by that. She was right—he was sorry he lived longer. She also had promised that she would wait for him, and Emma never broke a promise.

The ground was cold and wet and hard. All the things that made for a bad night's sleep and Quinn had a hard enough time sleeping in a real bed. The fish he'd eaten was just enough to remind his stomach how hungry he was. His poor gut was empty and making rebellious growling sounds. He'd not thought to bring food along. All he thought about was his destination. Food was always the last thing on his mind. After Emma died, the only time he ate was when he felt weak and knew he needed the energy. Like right now. Hell, anything sounded good to him right now, even Sugar's dog food. Bur he could never cheat his dog out of a meal. He still had a cigar and he liked to have a cigar after a good meal. Maybe he could convince his stomach that he'd just finished a large three-course meal and was topping it off with a good smoke. Anyway, he was hoping it'd take his mind off food.

He reached into his shirt pocket and pulled out his last cigar along with a book of matches he picked up at the bar the other night. On the front of the matchbook was a picture of a moose. He ran his finger across the face of the matchbook and tried to remember that night. It seemed so long ago, and he still wasn't clear what had happened. He opened the pack, broke off a match, struck it and held the flame to his cigar, inhaled and blew out the match with the smoke. He took a few drags off the cigar and laid back and looked up at a small break in the clouds and saw some stars for just a moment before the clouds filled in again. He started to rationalize what he was doing. He was trying to cross through these mountains and rivers to dump his wife's ashes in a creek. Did that sound like a smart thing to do? Not really.

He could be doing this because he knew he'd never make it and that might have been his intention all along. He wasn't sure. Hell, he wasn't sure about a lot of things these days. But sitting in that motel was something he could never do, and riding his horse, as always, was the only time he found any peace.

It started to snow again. The flakes were large and heavy as they floated down and began to cover him. Sleeping on the cold ground, when it's snowing, that was something else again. He might not even make it through the night. If he didn't make it, well, at least he wouldn't be hungry anymore.

He took one last drag off the butt of his cigar and tossed the stubby chewed-up end into the fire. He put his hat over his eyes and dozed off, but not for more than a few minutes at a time. The stiffness and ache in his legs kept waking him. He'd shake his legs and stretch and bend his toes. Then he'd lie back and try and think about all the good times he'd shared with Emma. He'd doze off again. Once he woke thinking he was hearing the whispering. This went on throughout the night, until early morning when he sank into a deep sleep.

The snow continued to fall the entire night. The fire slowly went out and was covered by a thick layer of fresh snow. Anyone looking down from above would never have seen Quinn's body. It would have appeared as just another clump of rocks. Quinn and Sugar were completely wrapped in a blanket of snow.

As it started to get light, Sugar wiggled her way out from under her new white blanket and shook the snow from her body. She started walking around smelling this unfamiliar new cold white ground. She finally came back to check on Quinn. She stuck her head into the snow and began licking his face.

Quinn raised his arm from under his slicker to push her away. He was surprised to discover he was still alive. Slowly he began to move his body and check his extremities to make sure everything was working. His hips hurt and his legs were so stiff he could hardly move them. He opened his eyes and squinted at his surroundings. It had stopped snowing but there was a thin layer of fog lying low to the ground. He was sore and his body was aching. He didn't want to get up, but he couldn't stand to lie there in pain any longer. He had to force himself to stand up. As he rolled over onto his hands and knees, the snow slid off his slicker onto his neck and back and down his jeans. He shivered and began pushing himself up into a standing position. Just to get to his feet seemed like a major accomplishment.

Quinn brushed the snow from his clothes with his hat, ran his hand through his hair, put his hat on and started walking around and stretching his legs, arms and his back. The more he moved about, the better he started to feel. He walked over to Bracket and swept the snow from his back. He seemed to have weathered the storm fine. Bracket held his head high, looking rejuvenated and ready to go. Quinn walked around looking for the trail that was hidden under the snow. When he found it, he followed it to the edge of the meadow, where it started to drop down into the thick fog. It would take them a while before they were ready to ride, and he was hoping the fog would dissipate by then.

"Where the hell is that dog?" He began looking around for Sugar and couldn't see her anywhere. It's hard to see a white dog in the snow. He called out her name, and looked and listened, but there was no movement or sounds coming from anywhere. It was all so quiet and still. He was getting anxious and kept calling for her. He couldn't believe she wouldn't come to him, that wasn't like her; since they had started this journey, she always stayed close by and never wandered off. He noticed that Bracket was acting restless. He went over to him and took off his hobbles and walked him over to a tree and tied him. Bracket was still jumpy and tossing his head and Quinn tried to calm him.

Then he heard a high shrieking sound. Quinn hurried in the direction of the noise. It was coming from behind some bushes. He pushed his way through to the other side, and there was Sugar, hanging from the mouth of a very large bobcat. Their eyes locked. Quinn yelled at the cat and threw his arms in the air and ran towards them. The bobcat dropped Sugar and took off. Sugar made an immediate turn and started barking and running after the cat.

Quinn shouted, "Sugar, Sugar, come back here, girl!" She stopped and turned around and started walking towards him. "You're a bigger idiot than I am! What were you thinking? That cat would've had you for breakfast." Quinn bent down and picked her up in his arms to make sure she was all right. Sugar's neck was soaking wet, and at first he thought it was blood. But it wasn't blood. It was saliva from the cat's mouth. He checked her all over, and there wasn't a scratch or tooth mark anywhere on her body. He couldn't find anything wrong; she was fine. The bobcat probably thought she was a lost cub and was taking her back to her den. "You're a lucky dog. You better stay close from now on. Who knows what else is hiding out there licking their chops over a pretty little thing like you. Well, there's no sense in us just standing around. I'll get everything packed up and we'll get on our way."

Quinn brushed down Bracket, then saddled him and picked up the campsite. The fire had gone out long ago from the snow fall. He tied his saddlebags and bed roll on the saddle, picked up Sugar and mounted his horse. He set Sugar in the sling, and they rode back through the meadow and across the small stream to where they had turned off the trail.

The trail was now covered in snow, but it was easy to follow along the hillside and around the trees that clearly marked its direction. Bracket stumbled once over a large rock that was hidden under the cover of snow, Quinn thought he was just being lazy and not picking up his feet. It was still early in the morning, and they weren't all awake yet, even with Sugar's early morning encounter. Quinn sat quiet in the saddle with heavy eyes half asleep. All he could hear was the snow falling from branches, the creak of the saddle and the crunching sounds of Bracket's hoofs pressing down on the snow. They kept following the trail as it worked its way down and around the mountain and through thick trees and across small streams and twice through heavy snow banks that nearly blocked the trail.

They finally caught up to the fog that Quinn had seen from their campsite. The fog was thick and dense and heavy. Quinn could barely see Bracket's ears, which were held alert. Occasionally, the fog would let up so that Quinn and Bracket could almost make out the trail, then they'd ride into another thick patch and be riding blind again. Quinn was growing uneasy and decided to get off and help lead Bracket through the worst parts. He held Sugar in his arms and the reins in his hand and slowly felt his way along. He was in no condition to be walking down rough mountain trails leading a horse and carrying a dog. Once he tripped over a tree root growing across the trail and went to his knees. He let go of Sugar and fell forward landing on his hands. Sugar stayed next to him; she had no intention of running off. While he was on his knees, Quinn could see under the fog and up the trail some distance. It looked clear and bright up ahead where the trail rounded a bend, so Quinn got to his feet and climbed back on Bracket with Sugar under his arm.

As they rode on, the fog began to dissipate, but snow was starting to pile up. The snow was two to three feet deep in some places, making it difficult to even find the trail.

They were on the side of a hill that curved around to their right. They kept going, staying close to the hillside, and as they reached the bend in the trail, it started to decline at a steep angle for about twenty-five feet.

Bracket stopped and looked down the snow-covered slope, not sure he wanted any part of it. Quinn stood up in the stirrups and looked over Bracket's head at the steep angle of the trail and felt the same way. "I think we can do this, boy," he said, trying to coax him along. "We have no other choice. This is the only way down." Quinn sat back down in the saddle and patted Bracket on his shoulder to show his trust in him. "Come on, boy, I know you can do it." Bracket hesitated, then cautiously took a first step then another and slipped, falling down on to his haunches. He slid all the way to the bottom, finally coming to a stop in a pile of snow that flew into the air and slowly drifted back down and covered them like a thin white sheet.

"Wow! That was some ride!" Quinn yelled out. Bracket jumped back up on his feet and shook his body. Quinn held on but almost dropped Sugar. They all got re-situated and continued down the trail with no further incidents. It had been a long time since his soul had felt this vibrant. He turned around and looked back up at the top of the slide they'd just come down and smiled.

At the bottom of the trail, they came to a flat area with a small stream running through it. On the other side the trail continued on up the mountain. Up ahead it broke off into two different directions. Quinn took out his map to double-check his location. He wasn't sure which way to go. The fork in the trail was not marked on his map. "Damn, I must have missed this somehow." The fog was above him now, and from below he couldn't tell which way the trails were going. He sure didn't want to take off in the wrong direction and find out later he'd have to double back. They had done enough riding without having to back track.

He decided this would be a good place to stop and rest. They could all use a break. He'd wait awhile for the fog to lift so he could distinguish the direction of each trail. There was only one right way.

He was beginning to get a funny feeling in his stomach that he might be getting himself lost. The thought of being lost in the mountains without food brought back stories from his childhood that had scared the hell out of him at the time. He was an old man now, and the stories still left a bad taste in his mouth. The stories told of people eating their dogs and horses in order to stay alive. He didn't think he could ever do that. He had one more can of dog food left for Sugar, and that was it. Maybe he should hold that out for himself. He wasn't sure about that, either.

Quinn let Bracket drink from the stream while he filled his canteen. He was tired and hungry and would kill for a cup of coffee. He went over to a large bolder and sat down and put his back up against the cold stone and shut his eyes. "Emma, do you remember when we use to go riding into the mountains and we would have so much fun laughing about silly things that we thought were so funny at the time? We always had our special trails to ride where we could be alone and when we were alone together it was the best. You wouldn't like this ride; it's not any fun at all, even though sometimes I feel you're with me. There is no more fun. I think I'm going crazy, Emma. I don't know why but I keep thinking I'm hearing voices." He mumbled all this in a low, soft voice. "Emma, do you think I'm going crazy?"

He thought he had been alone too long with just his dog and his horse. They didn't care if he was hearing voices or if he was crazy. They were just there with him at this time and this place, and that was all that mattered. He sat there for a long time, not moving. His thoughts turned into sleep and he slept there with knees up and arms crossed on his knees and his head on his arms for almost an hour. As the fog began to lift, his body began to warm.

He lifted his head, and he could clearly see the path laid out before him. He looked at his hands, which were dry and cracked. He rubbed his hands through his thinning hair and felt the stubble of his beard. He reached over and picked up his hat, placed it on his head and slowly got to his feet, sweeping the dirt from the seat of his pants with his open hand. Sugar had been by his side the whole time, still a little nervous about straying too far. Bracket was standing in the stream, eating the fresh green grass that grew along its edges.

Quinn picked up Sugar and walked over to his horse. Putting his hand on Bracket's nose, he gathered up the reins, pulled up on the latigo and tightened the cinch, then climbed into the saddle. They rode up the stream and crossed over between some thick trees growing along both sides of the trail. He kept thinking about the whispering, that haunting spirit that kept teasing him day and night. But once they left the stream and climbed up the trail, the fog began to lift, and his mind began to clear. Soon the fog was gone and beneath the partly cloudy sky, the day began to warm. Maybe the weather was on their side for a while.

He rode out of the trees and along a ridge where he could see over the tops of the forest and hills and the expanse of country to the east. It was crystal clear now, with only patches of light fog hiding in the trees below him. It seemed he could see forever. He stopped and pulled his boots from the stirrups, stretched his legs out and drank in the beauty of the land that spread out before him. Off in the distance he could see the valley of Bear Creek. Somewhere down there was the cabin. It all seemed so far away. He turned and looked to the north and could see the approximate location of the small lake and where the creek begins. It looked closer.

They were tired and needed more than a short rest. He was thinking that he should go directly to the cabin and relax. They could all eat their fill and get some much-needed sleep, then make a fresh start in a day or two. Or he could push himself, take the ashes up first, and then it would all be over at once.

He was bone-weary and the more he thought about it, the better the cabin, food and sleep sounded.  After all, he wasn't on the clock, and he didn't have to be anywhere at any given time.

He was on his own time.

# CHAPTER EIGHT

Quinn stepped down from his horse, dropped the reins, and set Sugar on the ground. He walked up a ways to the edge of the trail and looked up at the sun, now high overhead. He stared off to the East in the direction of the cabin. He couldn't stop thinking about her. Quinn shook his head and mumbled to himself, "I've come this far, I can't quit now."

He walked back to his horse, picked up Sugar, gathered up the reins and mounted. He was wasting time. They had to get moving; the day was not going to wait for him. Quinn decided to take Emma's ashes first and have it all over and done with. It was mostly downhill to the river, so they should move along at a pretty good clip.

It took him most of three hours to reach the river. It was an uneventful ride; Quinn even nodded off at one point and then only stopping once to rest. As he rode down the last hundred yards through a grove of budding Aspens, he could hear the rushing water long before he saw it. The sound was so loud he feared he had made a big mistake by coming here first. When they stepped off the trail onto the rocky shore, he could see immediately how extremely turbulent the river was running. It was wild; crashing over rocks and boulders and faster and higher than he'd ever seen it before. Entering the river and attempting to cross under these conditions terrified him. The river was only seventy-five or eighty feet across, but the current was strong and churning the water in all different direction.

Quinn rode up along the riverbank, hoping to find a more tolerable place to enter and cross to the other side, a place where the river would give them a pass and wouldn't punish them. He was getting weaker, and there wasn't a lot of fight left in him. He circled back, watching the rapids as he went. This was normally where they would cross, but that was later during the year when the river ran quiet and had lost its anger. Quinn sat on his horse, trying to judge the current. He stared down at the fast-moving water with its bright greens and whites and gold and dark blues all changing in a flicker of an eye as the river swept by, teasing him to enter at any time and at his own risk. The rocks on the bottom were round and worn smooth by hundreds of years of the constant onslaught of rushing water. They were slippery and would roll from under you when stepped upon. Quinn was worried that if Bracket slipped on the rocks in this deep water and went under, they'd all be swept away.

He sat and stared and watched and waited with no fear for himself, but he didn't want to endanger his horse or dog. It wouldn't be right. They were innocent, it wasn't about them, but the river didn't care. It would sweep all three of them away and never think a thing about it.

Quinn was breathing heavy now, trying to build up his courage, as once they started there was no going back. He would never be able to turn Bracket back in that strong current, and if they got caught twisting around it would all be over.

"That's it," he said, "We're going." He readjusted Sugar high up on his chest and made sure she was securely fastened. He wasn't much for waiting around. He knew he had to get this over with and the sooner the better.

He turned Bracket toward the river and spurred him, yelling out, "Go to hell, you raging bastard!" Bracket leaped out into the river with a vengeance. The water came up over his shoulders as they started working their way to the center of the river. The current became stronger as the river got deeper and began swinging Bracket sideways. Quinn legged him over as they came to a group of large rocks hidden beneath the swelling waves. Bracket stepped on one but his hoof slipped off and his head went under. Quinn was thrown forward out of the saddle and almost flew over Bracket's head but managed to hold himself firm with a tight grip on the horn. He leaned back and pulled up on the reins and raised Bracket's head out of the river. Bracket reared up, his legs slashing out at the water in front of him, then, holding his head high above the current, he leaped forward.

They were in the middle of the river now, and the water was getting deeper. They were swimming; Bracket's hoofs searching for a foothold. The rushing water was sweeping over the saddle, reaching as high as Quinn's chest. As the water surged up, breaking against his body, Sugar was forced up out of the sling and started to drift away in the current. Quinn could see her helpless expression as she glanced back, then she was gone, gone under, gone where? Quinn flailed his arms wildly, hoping to snag a leg, her tail, anything. Jesus, what have I done, he thought, I've killed her. He kept Bracket's head up and pointing towards the riverbank as he leaned over and stretched out feeling under the water. Finally his fingers grasped Sugar's tail. Holding tight, he pulled her up and scooped the limp white body into his arms. She started shaking and coughing up water, the current pushing them back into that deep pool of emerald-green water.

Bracket finally got a grip onto something solid and started pulling himself forward. Again he slipped off but reached forward once more for another try. Quinn could feel Bracket's massive muscles flex and stretch under him as the determined animal kept giving everything he had to reach the shore. Bracket, refusing to give up, continued to struggle as the river fought against him. Quinn kept yelling encouragement and pushing him forward. "Go! You can do it!" he yelled.

Bracket stepped forward onto a solid group of rocks that held and began to pull himself out of the current. They had made it past the center of the river. Approaching the other side, Bracket, with all the power he had left, made one final leap from the river onto the rocky shore. Quinn fell awkwardly from the saddle, landing hard on the rocks. Sugar jumped out of his arms, and Bracket kept running and bucking on up the trail and out of sight.

Quinn lay on his back, his eyes closed, not moving. He didn't know if he was alive or dead. He could hear the river, but it sounded far away. His body ached. He was dead tired, exhausted. Sugar came over to him and rested her head on his chest. The sun felt good on his cold wet body as he lay there on his back with the rocks as a mattress. He thought he might have passed out at one point. He wasn't sure about the time or how long he had been there. Events from his past kept flashing through his mind one after another. They were all scattered fragments of his life, and none of them seeming to fit together. Sometimes a bit of his past would flash by with the whispering voice not making any sense. "What am I missing?" he thought and his mind would go still again.

He felt a wind, something in the air, a flutter, a faint breeze. It paused and then again, a steady, warm breath on his face. Slowly he opened his eyes and squinted. Everything was hazy and a blur.

He blinked his eyes trying to focus on what was before him. Looking back, he saw Bracket standing, looking down at him, his nose an inch from his face. Startled, Quinn blinked his eyes again then opened them wide and he mumbled, "Oh, so you decided to come back did you? Probably not a wise decision on your part but I'm glad you did."

Slowly he pulled himself up onto his elbows and gathered in his surroundings. Then he struggled to his feet, his legs wobbling. Holding out his hand to steady himself, he looked down at Bracket's legs. There was a jagged cut below his left knee. The blood had started to cake up and dry but was still oozing. He held Bracket's head under his arm and put his hand on his neck; his body was quivering. He rubbed Bracket's neck and shoulder with his hand as he talked to him, "Good boy, you're going to be all right."

Quinn felt light-headed. Looking up in the air, he took a deep breath and let it out slowly. His clothes were still wet from the river and his feet squished in his boots when he took a step. He stood there holding on to Bracket, and a chill came over him as he thought about crossing that same river yet again.

Quinn bent down on one knee to get a better look at Bracket's legs. There was the one deep cut, a few scrapes on his knees, and he was missing his right front shoe. Quinn took a small neckerchief out of his back pocket and wrapped it securely around the cut on Bracket's leg. He wasn't sure how long it would hold, but it was the best he could do for now. Bracket held his head down, and Quinn knew the body language. He was about done in, and Quinn wasn't sure how much more he could get out of him. "I can't do it without you. I'd never make it up that hill."

Quinn turned, quickly looking around. "What? Where are you?" He heard the whispering again, and this time he could hear the words. "You're always in a hurry," the voice said, "There's plenty of time."

That didn't make any sense; he didn't have plenty of time. He hadn't eaten in two days. He was hungry and tired and if he didn't get this done soon it would never get done. He was confused, not understanding what was going on. Maybe he was delirious from hitting his head on the rocks when he fell from his horse.

He looked over at Sugar, who was lounging half asleep on a nice warm rock in the sun. Quinn thought about leaving her there and picking her up on the way back. But, after the attack by the bobcat, he thought better of it. Quinn called for her. She looked up and slowly walked towards him. Down river he spotted his hat stuck up against a piece of driftwood. He limped over, bent down and retrieved it. Slapping it against his leg, he put it securely on his head. He moved slowly back to his horse, trying to work the kinks out of his back. He stooped down one more time to pick up Sugar, who sat waiting, then took up the reins and led Bracket over to a large boulder so he could stand on it to mount. His body was worn out and he needed help getting on his horse and holding the dog at the same time. When he finally slid into the saddle, Bracket stood his ground so Quinn could adjust himself and Sugar for the ride up the final hill to their destination.

So this was it, the final leg of their trip to the green meadow, at the top of the hill where the creek started and where this whole adventure began all those years ago. This trip didn't start with a broken-down truck and trailer. It had begun over fifty years ago with Emma and her father, and now it was up to Quinn to end it and complete the final link. He stopped thinking about why he was doing this. It was just something he had to do.

The first half of the trail was clean and clear of debris, which made it easy for Bracket to move smoothly without exertion. Quinn knew this was too good to be true. Then he saw why his horse had decided to come back. He had hoped it was Bracket's concern for his well-being, but as it turned out it was the fact that the trail was basically gone. It just ended. He couldn't go any farther. The trail had been completely washed away by heavy rain. There were tree limbs down everywhere with no sign of any trail of any kind anywhere. The rain had loosened rocks and dead trees and swept away the trail along with half the hillside.

This trail had never been heavily traveled. Not many people knew about its existence. When people came here to camp and fish, they would always stay on the other side of the river where the ground was flatter and less demanding.

Quinn stopped and let Bracket rest while he sized up the situation. There weren't a lot of choices. He was going to have to make his own trail, bushwhack his way through to the top. He looked up searching for the large rock that marked the location of the meadow. Quinn patted Bracket on the shoulder, "Okay boy let's get this done."

They started slowly traversing back and forth, making long passes, first one direction across the side of the hill, then turning back in the other direction, inching their way along, stepping over dead trees and around rocks and boulders, climbing higher and higher on the mountain. Every once in a while, they would come across part of the old trail, but in the next moment it was a guessing game again. Bracket fought his way through branches and tree limbs and kept trudging along. The poor guy was really tired and was starting to wind down. More and more often, they'd stop and rest, and then Quinn would gently coax the horse on a little further.

By the time they made it to the top, Quinn's head was spinning, his legs were aching and his body was limp. He had no strength left as he bent over in the saddle and let Sugar slide out of his hands to the ground, then he fell from the saddle. He landed on his side and rolled over into a sitting position. They were all exhausted, and his memory was starting to play tricks on him again. The fatigue and hunger blurred his thoughts. He couldn't remember the reason why he was there, at that place.

Then he felt a warm wind blow through the Aspens, fluttering their leaves and awakening his mind. The ashes, he had Emma's ashes with him. The ashes were the whole reason for being there. He looked around wondering what he was to do next. He should get the ashes; they would tell him what to do. Once he held the ashes in his hands, it would all become clear to him. He struggled to his feet and over to Bracket, who was feasting on the tall grass just a few feet away.

He unbuckled the saddlebag and reached inside. He felt around, and his hand touched something cold and hard, like steel. He had forgotten about it, and all this time it was just sitting there waiting for him. He pulled it out and held it up to the sun, which gave it a rich golden glow. He smiled and sat back down on the ground, caressing it with both hands. "Now this will make everything right." He held it up to his lips, opened his mouth, tilted his head back and took a slow swallow. The whiskey burned at his throat and began to warm his body. "Oh my God, just what I needed." He'd take a drink, then set the bottle between his legs and look around as if he'd never been there before. He drank slowly from the bottle, and each time between drinks, he screwed the top back on as if he were afraid he might spill this precious fluid.

Quinn stared off into the distance, not moving, as if his brain had gone on vacation and he was in a trance. He was lying on a warm, sandy beach on a clear, sunny day. Emma was next to him and they were holding hands.

"Are you sure it will work?" Quinn asked.

"I'm positive it will work." Emma said, "Dad told me all about it, and he said it never fails."

"Okay, let's go give it a try." Quinn picked up their diving masks and they walked down to the clear blue water of the bay. They stood close together, knee deep in the warm water, looking down at the colorful fish as they swam around their feet.

"Now remember, honey, don't do anything until we swim out a ways over by the rocks."

"Okay, I'll follow you."

They dove in and started swimming towards the rocks. They each had a small plastic bag in their hands, full of frozen peas. When they got out to the deeper water around the rocks, they dove down looking around for the fish but only saw a few, here and there. Emma looked at Quinn and nodded. They reached into their bags, pulled out a handful of peas and spread them through the water. Within a second there were hundreds of multicolored fish of every shape and size, feeding in a frenzy all around them. Quinn started laughing and had to come up for air. He was coughing out water.

Emma popped up next to him with a big smile on her face. "See, I told you it would work." They looked back down in the water, and all the fish where gone. They'd vanished as fast as they had appeared.

"Where the hell did they come from?" Quinn asked. "And where did they go?"

"I don't know but that was pretty crazy wild wasn't it?"

"I've never seen anything like it. They just came out of nowhere."

"Sorta scared you at first, didn't it?" Emma said, still holding her bright smile.

"Yeah, I didn't know if perhaps when they finished with the peas they might start on us."

Quinn snapped out of his reverie. He looked back down at the bottle, opened it again and took another drink. He sat there for maybe twenty minutes, just nursing the bottle. He was starting to feel better. At least he thought he was. He put the cap back on the bottle, got to his feet and almost fell. He bent over and put his hands on his knees to steady himself. He stood up straight, took a deep breath and, his legs quivering, and started walking back to his horse. He opened the saddlebag again and this time found Emma's ashes. He lifted them out slowly, handling them with care. After all, this was his world, his life and his only love.

Holding the bag securely in his hands, Quinn turned around and looked over at the rocky ground where water was bubbling up out of the earth and started off, limping as he went along. When he got to the slippery rocks, he stumbled and fell, landing hard on his elbows. Blood started running down his arms, to his fingers, and began dripping off the bottom of the bag. He didn't look and he didn't care; he didn't even feel the pain. He struggled back up onto his feet and continued to labor his way across the uneven rocks.

When he reached the mouth of the creek, the sound of the water was loud and the power of it rushing up from underground made him unsteady, and he fell again. This time, as he was falling, the bag slipped from his hands and disappeared between the rocks. Stretching his arm down between the rocks, he touched the bag with the tips of his fingers, then stopped and lay there listening. He thought he heard whispering again, or was it the rushing of the water? No, it wasn't whispering, it was a voice this time. He was hearing her voice, and the words were clear. He could feel her presence, and he knew she was there with him.

"I'm so glad you're here, I need your help," he said. "I can't do this alone." He turned his head and looked back behind him, but she wasn't there.

"It doesn't matter," the voice said, "Leave them."

"No, I'll get them." He told her as he slid his hand further down between the cracks of the rocks and finally was able to secure the top of the bag with his fingers. "Please, don't leave me," he said, now confident he had rescued her ashes from the crevice, he began pulling them up. Then the bag snagged on something. He gave it a tug and the bag ripped open, and the ashes started spilling from the bag and slowly trickling back down between the rocks, out of sight.

Quinn's eyes filled with tears and he started to cry as he pulled up the empty bag. In a rage he crunched it up in his hands. He stood up on the rocks at the mouth of the creek and yelled at the top of his lungs. He looked up in the sky feeling pain and anguish and threw the bag as far as he could down the creek. "I'm just a stupid old man," he said out loud. "After everything we went through to get here, and then I fucked it up."

Quinn wanted Emma to hold him in her arms and comfort him. He wanted her to wipe his tears away and tell him how proud she was of him. But this could never happen now. Her ashes were scattered through the cracks of the rocks, and they would never make it to the creek to be with her father's. How was he ever going to live with this? His last promise he ever made to his wife and he can't deliver.

"Listen to me, Quinn," he heard the voice say, "My ashes are where they should be. The rain will wash them into the creek. You have to let go. I don't want you to grieve for years. Not like I did for my dad, wasting away precious life when there is so much to live for. That's why you're here. If you listen and follow your heart, your life will flow in the right direction. You followed your heart. You could have turned back but you didn't. You will never grieve as before, only sweet memories that will last forever, and your life will start again. I'm right here. I've been here all along. I love you. I have always loved you. Now it's time for you to start living again."

Quinn sat there his face in his hands, tears running down his cheeks. Was Emma really there talking to him or was it all in his exhausted head? Whatever it was, no one would ever convince him it wasn't Emma who had picked him up and set him down in the right direction. Sometimes you just know what's real and you don't have to explain it. He sat there for a long time, just letting his mind wander. She was right. The rain would wash her ashes into the creek. He kept hearing over and over in his head, the rhyme, "Ashes, ashes, we all fall down."

He had done what he started out to do; it was over. He had given his word and fulfilled his promise. Now it was time to go home and rest to start living again.

He slowly got up onto his feet and walking over to Bracket. He called out for Sugar and she came running. He picked her up and held her in his arms. He looked her in the face and asked, "You heard her too, didn't you?" Sugar started licking the dried salty tears from his cheeks and he knew that Emma's dog had also heard her.

He looked down and saw the whiskey bottle still sitting on the ground right where he had left it. He bent over to pick it up, took one final drink, then slipped the empty bottle in his saddlebag.

# CHAPTER NINE

Quinn took one last look around the hidden meadow; at its bright green grass, the reflecting lake and the surrounding aspens about to give birth. And as he tightened up the cinch he glanced over toward the spring, hoping to hear her voice once more before they rode off. The only sound he heard was the breeze blowing gently through the trees, and in the distance, the murmur of the bubbling creek. There was no whispering or voices.

He picked up Sugar, mounted Bracket and headed towards their new trail they made on the way up. His thoughts now turned to the river and how they were going to make it across without losing their lives. When they reached the shoreline, he stopped and looked out over the river and began trembling at the thought of taking his horse back into that turmoil. He was determined to find a more peaceful place to cross, a place where the river would not erase the good feelings he had or the memory of her voice.

They couldn't go down stream because of the high cliff that formed the deep pool of swirling water. They'd have to maneuver their way up river to find a crossing. Quinn turned Bracket and putting his heel to him, started working their way along the river. He had no idea how far he'd have to travel before he'd find a place to his liking. He was unfamiliar with this side of the river but one thing he knew for sure, he was going out of his way in the wrong direction and would eventually have to double back once they crossed to the other side.

The shadows were getting longer; he had to hurry, it would be dark soon, and he didn't want to spend another cold night sleeping on the hard damp ground. The weather had held, and there was no sign of rain or snow, but one more night without food or sleep was not something he was looking forward to. They rode up river, sometimes on the hillside high above the river, where he could see it twisting and turning, and other times on the rocky shore next to the river itself. There were no trails, so he just felt his way along. They climbed onto the hillside through heavy growth. He held his arms up and his head down protecting himself from branches and twigs that slapped him across the face and arms as he rode through whatever the forest laid out before him.

They had gone about a mile or so when he noticed the river becoming wider as it made a sweeping bend to the west. It looked to be seventy-five or hundred yards across. The water cascading over the stones, told him the river was shallow and made for an easy crossing. He stopped and sat watching, studying the current and looking for any signs there might be deep hidden holes he should avoid. He was running out of time. He had to cross the river soon and head back to the cabin before night overwhelmed them. If he got stuck riding in the dark, where there were no trails, they could easily get lost. He decided to cross here and now. Bracket was understandably hesitant at first, stopping to observe the situation for himself before stepping off into the river.

Guiding his way through the steady current, Bracket stumbled a few times but never lost his footing or direction, and the water never got deep enough to sweep them away. Slowly they worked their way across the still-angry river until finally they climbed out on the other side.

Bracket had lost another shoe to the river. Quinn stopped on the riverbank and dismounted to check on the condition of his hooves. The outside edges were beginning to break away. He unbuckled his saddlebag and grabbed the roll of duct tape he carried for just this kind of problem. He moved around in front of Bracket, bent down and picked up the right front leg. Holding the hoof between his knees, he wrapped the tape several time around the hoof for support, then set it back on the ground. He performed the same temporary fix on the other hoof. It should hold until they get back to the cabin where he'd nail on new shoes. All this time Sugar sat and watched with great interest until Quinn reached down to scoop her up. As he climbed back in the saddle, he took one last look at the crossing and shook his head, then laid the rains on Bracket's neck and turned him down river.

They moved out at a slow jog along the shore then off the beach up into the trees, where they found an old trail and followed it through the thick forest. When they came out of the trees, Quinn stopped and looked across the face of the canyon wall a hundred feet above the river. He pushed Bracket forward out onto the narrow, rocky path and rode across the face of the cliff, hesitant to look down, then back into the trees on the other side to the old familiar trail. They rode on for a short distance before it dropped back down to the rocky shore where they had made that torturous crossing earlier in the day. He stood for a moment observing the river. It gave him a chill, then knowing it was all behind him, he turned his horse away from the river and moved him on up the trail back into the mountains.

It was almost an hour before they came to the final trail that would lead them to the cabin. Quinn's thoughts kept drifting back to the spilled ashes in the rocks and the sound of Emma's voice and the words she had said to him. It was all so clear and exact. He knew she was right there next to him, and it made him feel safe and warm and longing to just feel her touch once more.

After a few miles he could feel Bracket favoring his right front leg. They had made it to a dirt road where there were a few cabins set back on the hillside. This road led to a small narrow bridge under which Bear Creek flowed. After crossing the bridge, they'd ride down stream alongside the creek for about two hundred yards to the cabin. Quinn stopped. He had to give Bracket a break. The poor guy had carried them long enough; he and Sugar could walk the rest of the way. Quinn stepped down from the saddle, stretching his limbs, and set Sugar on the ground. His legs were stiff and sore, reminding him how long he'd been in the saddle.

The three of them were tired and near broken as they walked the last few miles in the dark. After crossing the bridge over Bear Creek, Quinn could see the silhouette of the cabin against the cool gray starlit sky. When he turned off the road to the cabin, he went directly to the corral and unbuckled the breast collar, released the cinch and let the saddle fall to the ground. He opened the corral gate, slipped off the headstall and turned Bracket out. Quinn latched the gate and limped over to the porch. He slid his hand along under the porch joist to find the nail that held the cabin's key. Sugar was sitting by the door as he stumbled up the steps and unlocked it. It was dark and cold inside. He didn't turn on the lights but went directly to the bedroom, leaving the cabin door wide open. Quinn collapsed onto the bed and fell into a deep sleep.

It was late morning, around eleven o'clock, the sun streaming through the window and shinning on Sugar, who was lying next to Quinn on the corner of the bed. Quinn thought he was dreaming as he woke to the smell of bacon cooking and sat up in bed, his stomach begging for food. Quinn rolled over, put his feet on the floor and slowly pushed himself up. His body was stiff and sore. It took all his effort to take a few small steps to get moving. Stretching kinks out of his back, he walked into the kitchen to see Anna standing at the stove turning bacon with a long fork.

She looked over at him and smiled, as he stood at the kitchen door, trying to look innocent. "I'll bet you're hungry. Though I had doubts you were ever going to wake-up."

"Yeah, I'm starving. In fact it was the smell of your bacon that woke me or I would still be sleeping."

"We got worried when we didn't hear from you."

Quinn didn't say anything he just went over and sat down at the table. Anna brought him a cup of coffee. He took a few sips, trying to think how to explain why he hadn't called. But he knew... all he had were lame excuses. The truth is, he was in a mess and just forgot... until it was too late.

"Well... I'll have your breakfast ready in a few minutes." He could tell she was upset with him, and she had a perfect right to be. She and Rob had driven all the way to the cabin worrying that something terrible had happened. Quinn felt awful putting them through that pain. But then Anna could never stay mad at her dad for long. She was just glad to see him safe. "How do you like your eggs?"

"Anyway they come out is fine. But first, let me take a quick shower and get out of these dirty clothes. This is all I have with me. The rest of my things are in my truck. That's another story I'll have to fill you in on."

"I'll throw your clothes in the wash." Anna said, "I think there's a pair of sweats in the bottom drawer in your room. You can put them on until your clothes are dry."

When Quinn returned after his shower, his hair was combed and his three-day beard was gone. He was barefoot and wearing gray sweats. He came up to Anna and gave her a quick hug, then moved over to the table and sat down in his chair. Anna put his plate in front of him and he looked up. "You going to eat?"

"Rob and I have already eaten, you go ahead."

Quinn had a soggy business card in his hand and set it on the table next to his plate. He picked up his fork and began to eat, not like a man who was starving, but slowly tasting every bite, savoring every flavor, as if he had never tasted food before. After he'd mopped his plate clean with his buttered toast, he reached for the phone and dialed the number on the card. The phone rang four times before it was answered.

"You can call in the posse, I made it."

"Who is this?"

"It's the old man with the little white dog on the horse. We made it safe and sound, well mostly safe, anyway."

"Holy shit, you made it?" It was Bill Patrick, the ranger. "I would have given 10 to 1 you'd have come back and thought better of it."

"There were times when you came real close to winning that bet."

"I'm glad you called. Is everyone okay?"

"A few bumps and bruises, but we're fine."

"Your dog made it okay, too?"

"Well, she's not white anymore, more like a dirty brown with dreadlocks. I'll have to cut her hair off when we get home, but she's fine."

"Well, that's good news. I appreciate the call, and if you're up my way stop by and I'll buy you a beer and you can tell me the whole story."

"I'd like that." Quinn laughed and hung up the phone.

"Who was that, Dad?" Anna asked.

"That was the ranger who helped me map my way through the mountains. Nice guy."

Quinn looked up at Anna and he could tell she was about to cry. "What is it, honey?" He was surprised to see she was still upset.

"I've been so scared, I thought we had lost you too, and so soon after Mother. I just couldn't take that. It would destroy me if anything happened to you, too."

"Honey, I'm so sorry, it was wrong of me, and I should have called. I just forgot. I can only say I'm sorry so many times before the words become meaningless. I was being selfish. In trying to deal with my own grief, I never thought what I was doing to you and the family. I'm all right now and I want you to be all right, too. This trip has helped me in more ways than I could ever imagine, so no more worrying, okay? I'm going to be around for a long time. Maybe too long, and then you'll be trying to find ways to get rid of me." Quinn tried to end on a light note.

Robert came in from outside and got a cup of coffee and joined them at the table. He'd been busy turning on the well and checking the water lines. He found Quinn's saddle on the ground and put in the tack room along with his bridle. They all sat quietly. Robert and Anna sipped their coffee, their elbows on the table and their eyes on Quinn, not blinking, waiting for the words to come out. Waiting for him to explain what happen and how they all ended up together here at the cabin.

Quinn straightened himself up in his chair and cleared his throat and began to tell them about his trip. He told them about the heavy rain and taking the old road, his truck and trailer breaking down and the ranger and the trip through the mountains and the river. But he didn't tell them about the bar fight or the young girl who spent the night with him or the two boys who attacked him on the road or the farmer who shot at him in a field. Then there was the logging truck and, of course, the bobcat encounter—that all went unreported as well.

Quinn knew that Anna understood that there was more to the story than just the journey through the mountains, that he had had some special reasons for doing what he did, and that she'd never get the whole story out of him. Whatever it was, she sensed that it was personal between her mom and dad, and she could never fill in those blanks. Anna was no stranger to their life-long relationship. She'd seen it up close and personal. Quinn suspected that she envied their bond and connection to each other, just like so many of their friends did. They had been the quintessential couple. They played hard and loved hard. They were one. Anna knew him and whatever he was leaving out was all right, too, because he didn't need to tell everything. The main thing was, he had made it back safe and he was still with them. As for the rest, who knows, it might all come out someday.

Quinn also sensed that Robert was chomping at the bit and could hardly wait for the opportunity to make his evaluation of what went down. So Quinn pushed his chair back and got up from the table, excused himself and went to his room to put his clean dry clothes on. It was a small cabin where secrets were impossible, one of many things that Robert had yet to learn.

"The ol' fool never should have gone in the first place," Quinn heard Rob saying. "I told you it wasn't a good idea."

"You know Rob, I'm getting really tired of you calling my dad an ol' fool, he's anything but an ol' fool, it's just his way of keeping his life going and trying to move ahead in some kind of direction." Quinn could tell Anna was trying to keep her voice down and stay calm.

"Well, it's not a very smart direction, if you ask me."

"Nobody's asking you," she snapped back.

"Okay, okay, let's drop it, I'm sorry. I know he's been through a lot and it hasn't been easy for him. It's just that he should have told us, that's all."

"Well he didn't tell us, so let's just get over it."

"I'll say one thing for him. There's not many men his age that could have made that trip. I know I couldn't."

"Thank you," she said in a softened voice.

Quinn walked out of the bedroom, smiling broadly and looking like a new man, still old but clean and fresh and ready to start a new day that was already half over. Walking over to Robert and patting him on the back, Quinn beamed, "I know you have to get home. I just want you know how much it meant to me finding you both here this morning. When we came dragging in last night, it was dark and cold, there was no way I could have opened the cabin, the shape I was in."

"We were lucky there weren't any water leaks." Rob said.

"There's one more thing before you go. I'll need a hand when I stitch up Bracket's leg," Quinn said. "Then maybe I'll hitch a ride to town with you to pick up my truck. I'm thinking of staying up here for a few days and coming home next weekend. I want to rest Bracket before I put him in the trailer, and it will give me time to relax, too." He looked back and forth between the two of them, one more skeptical than the other. "I promise I won't do anything stupid... without calling you first."

They smiled at his attempt at humor and agreed it was a good idea for him to stay, and they hoped he'd keep his promise. Quinn still had a lot of things to do around the cabin. Things that Rob didn't have time to do. Anna also made Quinn promise to call once in a while during the day, just to check in and make sure he was all right. It was the least he could do after what he had put them through. He didn't want them to drive back up just because he forgot to call. So he wrote himself a large note and hung it next to the phone, just as a reminder. Notes are what you do when you start growing old.

When they drove down the mountain and into the parking lot at the auto shop, Quinn could see his truck and trailer in the back yard. The trailer looked to be level on the truck. A good sign it was fixed.

Robert pulled up in front of the office and parked. "We'll wait here and make sure it's ready."

Quinn felt uneasy letting them stay. He didn't want them to hang around in case Lloyd started any trouble. He didn't want them involved. "Okay, I'll run in and check. I'll be right back."

Quinn got out of the car, walked up to the office and opened the door. The owner was sitting at his desk when Quinn walked in. "Hi." Quinn smiled. "Remember me... and my broken-down truck trailer?"

The owner looked up from his desk and stared at him for a second, then said, "Yeah, it's all already to go."

"Great, I'll be right back. Just want to get rid of my ride."

Quinn hurried back to the car and opened the door and leaned in, resting his arm on the top of the car. "It's all ready. Thanks again for all your help; I'll be fine now, so I won't hold you any longer. Give my love to the kids. When I get back, I'll take you all out to dinner and tell you all about my great adventure, with plenty of exaggerations thrown in."

They laughed, and Anna turned and looked up at her dad. "Are you sure you're going to be okay?"

"I'm positive, honey. So stop your worrying."

"Alright, Dad, we'll see you next weekend, and don't forget to call."

"You really did save my life. I was so happy when I saw you."

She reached up and hugged him. Quinn closed the door and they drove off.

Quinn walked to the office and went inside. The owner got up from his desk and came over to the counter and said. "We finished her up yesterday."

"I'm ready to settle up my bill. How did it go?"

"Everything went fine. We had to do some welding, and we put a new jack on your trailer. The old one had busted off."

Quinn paid his bill with a credit card, and as the owner handed it back he looked Quinn in the eyes and offered some friendly advice "You might think about investing in a newer trailer if you're going to do any long hauling. Yours hasn't a lot of life left in it."

Quinn nodded. "Neither do I, but I'll take that under consideration."

"I'll have someone bring your truck around to the front. It will just be a few minutes."

Someone bringing his truck around, this could get interesting, Quinn thought. Should he be planning an offense or a defensive strategy? He had no idea what to expect, he'd just have to play it by ear.

Quinn was standing out in front of the office with the owner when his truck came around the corner of the building. He concentrated all his attention on the driver to see what his first move would be. He looked hard at the driver. He had never seen him before. He turned to the owner. "Don't you have a guy named Lloyd working here?"

"I did, but he's long gone."

"He's gone?"

"Yeah, he split town. The police came around looking for him. They had a warrant for his arrest."

"Arrest warrant? What for?"

"Battery."

"Battery! Did he beat up that little girlfriend of his?"

"No, but I hear she left town, too. Probably took off with him. Too bad, she seemed like a nice girl."

"So who got battered?"

"He beat the hell out of those two stupid kids he was running around with. I don't know why, but he just kicked the living shit out of both of them. Put them in the hospital. I heard young Joey might not make it."

"Oh my god, he beat them that bad?"

"Yeah, he's a bad ass son-of-bitch. I thought I was helping him when he got out of jail by giving him a job. He said he was trying to turn his life around. I guess some guys are just born bad."

Quinn thanked the man for fixing his truck, then got in and drove to the store for a few items before heading back to the cabin. He was feeling anxious for some reason. His mind kept wandering.

He couldn't stop thinking about the beating of those two boys. Was it because of him? He drove slowly on his way up into the mountains, not really seeing the road.

When Quinn got back to the cabin, he unloaded the bale of hay from his truck and tossed a couple of flakes to Bracket. He couldn't shake the uneasiness he was still feeling. Was it Emma?

So many things kept clouding his thoughts. He went inside the cabin and poured himself a stiff drink, then walked back out and stood on the deck looking off towards the creek on the far side of the pasture. He could tell it was running high, he could hear it, that constant rush of water roaring over the rocks. Then, as a deep sorrow swept over him, he thought of the ashes. Would it ever go away?

Quinn spent five more days at the cabin. He wanted to rest his horse and his dog and even himself before taking the trip home, home to an empty house. He tried to give Sugar a bath in the kitchen sink and brush out some of her mats, but that ended before it got started. Sugar growled at his attempt at untangling her matted hair and even snapped at him until Quinn quit, tossing her onto the floor in frustration. Sugar scurried outside through the open cabin door, and Quinn followed her onto the deck. He sat down in one of the chairs and called to her. "Come here, girl, I didn't mean to hurt you." Sugar immediately came back to him and sat at his feet, waiting for him to reach down and scratch her head. "I guess we'll leave the grooming to the pros."

During this quiet time alone, Quinn tried to reflect on more pleasant things he and Emma shared through the years, but couldn't hold onto his thoughts. As the days pasted he grew restless. And on the fifth day, he got up early, loaded Bracket in the trailer, put Sugar on the seat next to him and started the drive home.

# CHAPTER TEN

Quinn was home now, and the heavy weight of sorrow and grief was largely gone. He was starting over alone, trying to find a new life for himself, a life without Emma. It was like driving at night without headlights—you might reach your destination, but you'd miss so much along the way. The warning signs, the wrong turn in the road, the house you drove past, the one you were looking for. Life was changing in enormous ways. No more atta boys or come and look at this sunset or let's have a glass of wine and sit on the porch and talk. All little things, but all important to life that you don't think about until they're gone. The sadness was still part of his every day, but it wasn't the feeling of deep despair. No, it was something different now, something that would come and go, like a sudden warm breeze in the afternoon. He knew that it would always be there, usually during the quiet moments alone at night when his thoughts would turn to her. It's funny, he thought, how we only remember the good times, and it's hard to recall the feeling of pain once it's gone. Maybe it's God's way of keeping us from giving up on life after being dealt a bad hand.

Slowly Quinn began finding ways to fill his day. There was always work to be done on the one-acre property, work he had neglected for some time was now getting done. Never did he feel bored with what the day had planned for him; days, warm and sunny, when he'd sit outside on the porch and read in the afternoon, and days when he drove out to the ranch to spend time with his brother Will. When they were younger, they were never very close. Quinn was a lot older, and they never spent much time together. But as the years went by, they'd grown closer and became good friends. They liked to ride together around the ranch and to the places Quinn had loved as a child and a young man.

They talked about ranching and livestock and the good old days but especially about horses. Will was a much better rancher than Quinn had ever been. Quinn liked to play; and when he was in his late teens, some might say he played too much. On weekends there was always something, a rodeo he couldn't miss out on, and by the time he made it back home, it was sometimes the middle or end of the following week. Most times he was out of money, and even when he won an event, he managed to come home broke.

During the years of Emma's illness, Will was always there for Quinn; more than once he'd helped him through rough times, emotionally and financially.

Quinn's life seemed to be finding a new normal. He once again took his rides into the hills around his home. These rides were still the favorite part of his day. He often met up with his friend Joe Ried, who lived a mile or so east of his place. The two of them would ride side by side and talk about high school football and politics or just gallop their horses through the dry grass feeling young again.

Late one afternoon on a Thursday, after Quinn and Joe had parted company, Quinn rode on an hour or so longer, just Bracket and himself. It was later than usual when he finally turned up his street and started riding towards his house. The tall trees were now casting long dark shadows along the street in front of him, obscuring his vision. Quinn thought he saw a car parked out in front of his house. As he approached the car he noticed someone sitting in the driver's seat. Then suddenly the car started up and drove away. It seemed strange, but he'd seen strange things before, and he thought no more about it. He rode on up the driveway and around in back to the barn and put Bracket up then went into the house for the night.

That weekend he was invited over to his daughter's house for a family dinner and get-together with friends. This would be the first large gathering of friends and family since Emma's funeral. Quinn had mixed emotions about going. He was afraid it might bring up everything he had managed to fold away and secure in the drawer of his soul. Would it now be opened and presented to the public for all to see? At the same time he knew that Emma would want him to be there— after all, he was going to have to deal with being around people someday. Quinn couldn't continue to hide from life. He'd been spending too much time alone, and he knew it was wrong; even his friend Joe knew nothing about his real life. Sooner or later he was going to have to start living in the world of people. This safe night at his daughter's house was probably a good place to start.

Quinn managed to pull himself together and drive to Anna and Robert's home. He parked in the driveway and walked to the front door. He felt awkward and so alone not having Emma at his side. He'd never gone to any function alone before. Emma was the one who carried the conversation, and now he would have to fend for himself. He did remember to bring a bottle of wine. Good boy, he thought to himself, you're getting off to a great start.

Quinn rang the doorbell and waited nervously until Anna opened it with a big smile and a hug. "Come on in, Dad. You didn't have to ring the bell. There're a lot of old friends here who want to see you." She escorted him into the party. Quinn made the rounds and did quite well, holding onto his smile. He got a drink and settled down. It turned out to be a surprisingly fun and enjoyable evening. It was almost like the old days. It felt right that they could all talk and laugh about all their fondest memories of Emma, and he thought it was good for everyone to remember. It made him sad at times, but it was a pleasant sadness that he could relax and be comfortable with.

On his way home from the party, he couldn't stop smiling and thinking how Emma would have liked being there. He could still see her beautiful face and the hands that he loved to hold and feel her soft touch. Knowing that this would always be with him, Quinn smiled again, but more gently.

As he turned onto his street, Quinn once again noticed a car parked across from his house, and his headlights showed that someone was sitting in the car alone. He drove past the car and turned into the driveway, but by the time he stopped the truck and got out, the car was gone. "The second time this week," Quinn said. "Who the hell would want to stalk an old man?" He looked up at the vast starry sky as if searching for a familiar face. "Maybe I have a fan club and don't know it." He left it there and walked up onto the porch, but stopped and looked back over his shoulder before going into the house. If it happened again, he'd try to check the license number.

Quinn planned to go to the cabin on Thursday. It was the second week in October, and the weather was turning cold. They'd already had freezing temperatures during the night at the cabin, but so far no snow. It was his job to shut down the well, drain the water lines and put up the storm shutters, winterizing it for the year.

He'd drive up with his two wilderness companions, Sugar and Bracket. He would never go to the cabin again without them. They were now just part of the protocol.

107

Quinn packed up early on Thursday morning, and they left the house a little after sunrise. The weather was holding. It was cold, but the rain they had earlier in the week had moved on to the east and the day looked promising. He took the Interstate, he always took the Interstate now, there was no more driving on the old road—he'd take the trucks and traffic over the dips and shoddy roads. Two hours later, he came to the Melville turnoff and drove twelve miles past it to Highway 21, which took him up into the mountains on a twisting winding road. In an hour he'd come to a small village called Beaver Creek. He drove through the village to the first dirt road, turned right and drove northeast seven miles to Bear Creek and the cabin.

Quinn pulled up in front of the cabin and parked. He reached over and picked up Sugar, opened his door, leaned over and set her on the ground. A cold wind was blowing up from the east through the aspens and pines. The leaves of the aspens rattled in the wind as they tried to hold onto the last of their color. He stepped out of the truck, grabbed his jacket and slipped it on, quickly buttoning it up. Then reaching in the cab, he took his hat off the dashboard, ran his hand around the lining and put it on, pulling the brim down to secure it against the wind, and shut the door.

Turning towards the cabin, Quinn stopped and stared. Something wasn't right. He took a few steps forward and stopped again and listened, but all he heard was the wind, the cold wind blowing up against his back. Turning slowly, he looked all around. Nothing seemed to be out of the ordinary. He shook his head and told Sugar, who was at his heels, "I must be on edge after that long drive. Come on, let's get Bracket out of the trailer."

When Quinn backed Bracket out, his horse began to stomp at the ground and shake his head up and down. He must be jittery too after the long drive, Quinn thought, and placed his hand on the side of Bracket's neck to calm him. Then he walked him over to the corral, unlatched the gate and turned him out.

Quinn moved slowly along the corral fence to the cabin porch, up the steps and across the deck to the door, then suddenly stopped and took a step back. The door was slightly open. He turned his head and looked around for Sugar. "Sugar, where are you!" She came out of the cabin, wagging her tail, and looked up at him. Quinn bent down and picked her up then put his foot against the door and pushed it all the way open. Quinn never forgets to lock the cabin, someone broke-in. It's not unusual, in the mountains, for someone's caught out in a snow storm to break into a cabin for shelter, but there hasn't been any snow storms. Quinn walked through the cabin trying to see if anything was missing or out of place, but everything seemed fine as best he could remember.

It was cold in the cabin. Quinn went over to the large stone fireplace and began building a fire to cut the chill. As the fire took hold, he stepped back and noticed flickering reflections of the fire coming from behind the chair next to the wall opposite the fireplace. He glanced up at the wall above the chair. How could he have missed it? The photo of Emma on her horse Sammy was missing. He pulled the chair away from the wall, and there on the floor was the framed picture with the glass broken. He picked up the picture and removed the remaining bits of glass from the frame and hung it back on the wall. As he was cleaning up the broken glass, his body shivered with an eerie feeling.

He spent a restless night, but in the morning he went about his chores trying not to think about the strange occurrences. The day went by without any further incidents. With all this craziness, he was beginning to think maybe he was spending too much time in conversation with only his dog and his horse. That evening, as the sun was setting behind the mountain, he decided to take a short walk up the road and onto the small narrow bridge over Bear Creek. He stood there, leaning against the railing, looking down at the clear cold water as it flowed beneath him, wondering if Emma's ashes had reached that far yet. He stayed on the bridge for quite a while, remembering and listening to the sound of the water as it rushed over the rocks on its way downstream. It was quiet this time of year. There are very few people still around. Most of the cabins are already closed for the winter. Tomorrow he'll take Bracket for a ride and see who was still holding on. Maybe he could find someone who knows about his cabin being broken into, or had seen strangers wandering about.

By noon the next day, he had finished his work on the cabin; the only thing left was to drain the pipes and turn off the well. He'd do that the following morning and then leave for home. After his noon meal he went out and got Bracket. He brushed him, and put the blanket and saddle on then slipped the bit in his mouth, buckled the headstall and walked him over to the front porch. Sugar sat and watched as he prepared to leave. Quinn dropped the reins on the ground and picked up Sugar and put her in the cabin, shutting and locking the door. She'd be safe and would probably sleep while he was gone. He took up the reins, mounted his horse and rode off down the road, then up on the hillside, checking cabins as he went along.

He met up with a hearty middle-aged couple who spent the entire spring, summer and fall at their cabin and were contemplating trying to make it through winter. That seemed like a harsh idea to Quinn after his trip through the mountains last spring. But he thought they had as much a right to be stupid as he did. They had not seen anything unusual or any strangers. That seemed to be the recollection of every one he spoke to, which amounted to four other people.

He'd been out about an hour and a half and was on his way back when he heard Sugar off in the distance barking. The barking was constant, she never let up. He pushed Bracket into a lope and approached the cabin from the rear. As he rode around the corner to the front, he pulled Bracket to a sliding stop. He sat his horse and gasped at what he saw; from a rope above the steps up to the porch hung a dead deer. It had been dead for some time. There was no blood. Its carcass had been ripped open, and there were large open wholes in its head where the eyes once were. Quinn legged Bracket over next to the porch and took out his knife and cut the rope tied to the banister, and the bloodless carcass fell to the ground. He stepped out of saddle and picked up the end of the rope and got back on, dallied it around the horn and dragged the carcass off into the woods, where he dumped it.

What kind of crazy person would do something like this? Was it tied into the break-in and Emma's picture shattered on the floor? What the hell was going on around here? A bunch of kids playing practical jokes? Or something else? Quinn was having trouble keeping a sense of humor about it, but he had a feeling that, whoever did this wasn't trying to be funny. He was leaving in the morning and wouldn't be back for six months. He hoped that by then, whoever did this had gotten it out of their system.

In the morning, he got up early and was ready to leave by nine o'clock. There'd been a thunderstorm during the night, and there was still a light rain swirling around with a cold wind blowing down from the mountains to the east. Quinn loaded Bracket into the trailer and picked up Sugar and put her in the truck. Just as he was climbing in, he heard a cracking sound and a pop. He grabbed Sugar and ducked down behind the open door. A bullet came through the center of the windshield, about five inches above the dash, and embedded itself in the back of the seat. He held tight to Sugar as he looked over the top of the door, trying to see where the shot came from. "Shit, now someone's trying to shoot me?"

It was misty and hard to see anything through the light rain. He could tell by the angle of the bullet's entry through the windshield and where it ended up in the seat that the shooter must be up on the hillside, in the trees off to his left. He put Sugar on the floor and climbed in, staying low on the seat, shut the door and started the truck. He cut the wheel to the right and started forward, driving blind with his head down on the seat until he had the hillside at his back. Then he sat up, stepped on the gas and sped off around two trees. Bouncing up onto the dirt road, they took off with dust and gravel flying, the trailer fishtailing.

Quinn was sweating and his heart was trying to pound its way out of his chest. By the time he reached the paved road above Beaver Creek he'd calmed down and was breathing normally. His mind was going back over what just happened. He didn't want to believe that someone was aiming at him. There was no reasoning for that, but then there wasn't any reason for the other things, either. He never had a lot of friends, but he didn't think he had any enemies, none that he knew of, anyway. It was the middle of hunting season, he told himself, and it could have been a stray bullet. Quinn never believed much in conspiracy theories, but after this trip he was beginning to have second thoughts.

# CHAPTER ELEVEN

Three weeks later, after Quinn closed the cabin, he was working out in the barn cleaning the stalls when he heard Sugar barking from the house. He stopped what he was doing and turned and listened, wondering what was bothering her. The barking continued. Quinn leaned his rake up against the stall and decided to take a coffee break and quiet the dog at the same time. Opening the back screen door, he went into the kitchen and poured the cold leftover coffee into his cup and set it in the microwave.

Sugar was still barking as he walked into the living room at the front of the house. "What are you barking at girl?" He bent over, picked her up and looked out the window. And there was that strange car parked in front of his house again, with someone sitting in the driver's seat. Was it the same car? He wasn't sure. The first time he hadn't paid much attention to it, and the second time it was late at night and dark. It all seemed kind of weird, and Sugar sure didn't like it sitting out there.

He was trying to think of a way to get behind the car to check its plates. Maybe he should just go outside and confront the person face to face. But if he tried that, the guy would just drive away and he wouldn't get the license number.

Quinn went out the back door, crept around the side of the house and stopped at the corner. He could see the car clearly, but he needed to get closer to see the numbers on the plate. The car looked like a late seventies or early eighties Chevy Camaro. He could see the back of the driver's head but couldn't make out any facial features. It was a man, and he was looking straight ahead. Quinn had to get closer before the guy drove away. He climbed through a tall hedge that ran along his neighbor's driveway and walked to the street hidden by the foliage, but as he approached the car from the rear, it took off. Quinn stood in the street watching as it drove to the corner, turned and quickly sped out of sight. He managed to get a partial plate number before it drove away. The car was from Colorado. He turned and hurried back into the house to write the numbers down before he forgot them. There in front of him on a piece of paper was a badly scrawled name of a state and some numbers that meant nothing to him. What was he going do with a state and four numbers?

That night it kept eating at him. Quinn went back into the kitchen, picked up the scrap of paper and stared at the numbers. He wanted to tell someone and get their opinion, but he didn't want to worry anyone either. He didn't want people to think he was in danger or he was crazy and making something out of nothing. But he was curious, and it was just bugging the hell out of him.

Quinn finally decided to call Kim, Emma's oldest and best friend and a lawyer. She still handled some legal affairs for friends but most of her time now was spent caring for her elderly mother. Kim had long silver hair that hung down to the middle of her back, a left-over from her hippie days, and big brown eyes. She was about five foot four, cute, with a petite little figure. In court, to those who didn't know her, she looked like a pushover. But Kim was smart and quick, and her opponents usually found out much too late that this cute little pushover was unrelenting.

"Kim, I was wondering if you could help me with something."

"I'll try, what is it?"

"Well a ..." Quinn paused, not knowing exactly how to phrase his question, "Do you know any way to find out a person's name through their license plates?"

"You mean do I know how to run plates?"

"Yeah, I guess."

"No. What's going on? Why do you want me to run plates on someone?"

"Oh, it's nothing."

"It's not nothing or you wouldn't be calling. So what's going on?"

"Well...it's just that I keep seeing this strange car around, and I was wondering who it was, that's all."

"Are you in some kind of trouble?"

"No, it's nothing like that. I'm just curious to know who it is."

"Look, Quinn, if you're in some kind of trouble you can tell me. It won't go any further."

"I'm not in any trouble, honest, Kim. I'd tell you if there was something to tell. So can you do it or not?" He didn't mean to get short with her. He really hadn't wanted to call her in the first place, but he couldn't think of anyone else, and now that he had called her, he wished even more that he hadn't. He was afraid she was going to get more information out of him then he was willing to give. Kim was good at that.

"I'll see what I can do, but then you better tell me what's going on."

"Sure, once I know who it is, if there is anything to tell, I'll tell you. But I'm sure it's really nothing."

"Okay, what do you have?"

"They're Colorado plates but I'm missing the last two numbers. They're on an older Chevy Camaro."

"You're not making it easy but I'll see what I can do and call you when—and if—I get anything."

"Thanks Kim. I knew you would come through."

"Don't be so sure."

They said their goodbyes and hung up. A week went by with no sign of the car. Quinn was back to life as before and had almost forgotten about the car and his conversation with Kim. He had just finished his dinner when the phone rang. He got up from the table and put his plate in the sink as he picked up the phone. It was Kim, and she caught him by surprise.

"I have a name for you," Kim said in a straightforward lawyer tone.

"Boy, you are good at this." Quinn was starting to get nervous. He hadn't expected Kim to get back to him so soon or even at all.

"It seems your mystery driver is an ex-con by the name of Lloyd Blake." When she said the name, the hair on the back of his neck stood up and a cold chill went down Quinn's spine. Kim continued. "He seems to be a very violent person. There's even an assault and battery warrant out on him. Are you sure you're not in any trouble? This is not a nice guy."

"No, I never even met this guy, and besides I haven't seen the car since I first talked to you. He's probably left town by now. You know you're the first person I would call if I were in any trouble."

"You better not be putting me off on this one, Quinn. If there is something going on you better tell someone, if not me, the police."

"There's nothing going on. Like I said I just kept seeing this car, and now it's gone. So it's over. I'm sorry to have troubled you for nothing," he said, knowing Kim didn't completely believe him. They talked a little longer, and he left her with a polite thank you.

After they hung up, Quinn sat down and started to think about what might be going on in that crippled mind of Lloyd's. It sounded like Lloyd had a case of revenge and was just toying with him. "Shit, I'll bet that was him tormenting me at the cabin." It all made sense to him now. Lloyd was out to do him harm; he probably had Sugar on that list too. What an awful thought that was. He remembered his old gun out in the tack room; he'd better get it out just in case and keep it handy. He was worried. If Lloyd had gone through all the trouble to track him down, he was dealing with one sick son-of-a-bitch.

Back then, in the bar, when all that was going down, Quinn had had no fear of injury or death. He had so much rage in him at the time that he didn't care what happened. But things had changed, his life was better now—all that anger in him was gone. Now it was Lloyd who had all the fearless rage and Quinn knew the power that came with it. So Quinn was going to have to be real careful and think this through. He knew Lloyd hadn't left town and was still hanging around, waiting and watching for whatever time and place suited him.

Quinn was frightened now. He had better not do anything stupid because Lloyd knew exactly what he was doing.

Lloyd had his plans, and whatever they were, Quinn had to be ready.

How does someone prepare for something, when he has no idea what's coming? It was already playing with his mind. Maybe that's part of Lloyd's plan, to keep him on edge and slowly drive him crazy or until he becomes an easy target. "Hell, I'm already an easy target." Quinn said to himself. "I'm a sitting duck. He could have had me any time he wanted."

The first thing Quinn decided to do was leave the outside lights on at night. He knew if anyone approached the house, Sugar would bark. She was his alarm system.

116

Days went by and nothing happened, no car, no Lloyd, almost three weeks without a sighting. Quinn was beginning to think he'd gotten all worked up over nothing. But he could feel Lloyd was out there somewhere, somewhere waiting, waiting for the right time, the moment that meant something to him. It had to be in a special place, a special time, for Lloyd to get full satisfaction, and that could be any crazy time. Quinn knew he couldn't let down his guard. It could happen two minutes from now or two years from now. Even if he got thrown back in jail for some stupid thing like kicking a dog or driving with no taillight, he'd just get out again.

Quinn always thought he was as normal as the day is long. He had no idea what went on in the head of a crazy person like Lloyd. He admittedly might act a little nutty at times, but not psycho crazy like Lloyd.

The next day Quinn drove to the market. He had things to do and couldn't keep putting them off. Bracket hadn't been ridden in a week. Quinn thought he would take him out on a ride in the afternoon when he got back and take his gun with him. He was starting to carry the old .38 Colt everywhere he went.

On the way to the market, he drove past a strip mall and at a glance he thought he saw Lloyd's car parked in front of a sports bar. Without even thinking, Quinn made a quick left turn across oncoming traffic into the parking lot. A car had to slam on its brakes to keep from hitting him. The man driving yelled out his window at Quinn and gave him the finger wave. Quinn waved an apology as his truck shot into the parking lot and came to a screeching stop. He sat in the cab and caught his breath. That was stupid. Quinn said to himself, I almost got killed. If I keep acting this crazy, I won't have to worry about Lloyd.

Quinn glanced around before driving through the parking lot to check out the car he thought was Lloyd's. He drove past it and without stopping, looked at the plates. Sure enough, it was Lloyd's car. He drove two rows behind Lloyd's car and parked the truck and sat there for a few minutes, twisting his hands back and forth on the steering wheel nervously, and thinking about what he was going to do next. He should go on his way. He knew this wasn't a very smart thing for him to be doing. But it was something he had to do. He needed to see the face of the person who was trying to kill him. Quinn sat and thought of what ifs and played them over in his head. He's not a young kid and he's not playing a private detective in a movie. This is real life and he's an old man, that doesn't move very fast and his eyesight's not the greatest. Although he did spot the car in the parking lot, that's one thing to his credit. As his mind kept darting from one thought to another, he grew angry with himself, and his patience were wearing thin. I'm going in there and tell off the little bastard, he told himself, I'm sick of him hanging around.

Quinn got out of the truck, still not sure if he was being stupid or smart, and walked up to the door of the bar, turned his head to see who was around, and put his hand out to open the door but stopped. If he opened this door, Lloyd would spot him before his eyes adjusted. Quinn dropped his hand to his side. He began to get cold feet. He started moving slowly towards the end of the building.

He walked past a small antique store and an animal clinic to the corner of the building, turned into an alley and went around to the back. There were a few cars parked in back, and there was a long wooden fence that went the full length the alleyway behind the building. Up against the back fence, spaced out evenly, were three large trash dumpsters. Quinn started moving slowly long the back of the building and stopped at the third door. It opened, and a man stepped out carrying a large cardboard box heading towards a dumpster. Quinn reached out and held the door for him and glanced inside. The man nodded thanks. Quinn took his hat off, wiped his brow with the back of his hand and stepped through the doorway into a dark hall. He walked along the wall, passed the restrooms that smelled of vomit and entered into a poorly lit bar.

It wasn't real dark inside, but it took time for his eyes to adjust. There were six people sitting at the bar, but he didn't think Lloyd was one of them. He saw an empty stool at the far end next to the wall. Quinn kept his hat in his hand and worked his way along behind the patrons who were all talking and seemed to know one another and asked if the stool near the wall was taken. The man sitting next to it said, "It's all yours." Quinn sat down, put his hat on the bar and ordered a beer. There were two TV screens over the bar and a large room behind him with tables and chairs, and beyond that were pool tables and more TV screens of various sizes.

Quinn took a sip of beer and started to think. He wasn't real sure who he was looking for. It'd been almost a year since the incident in the bar, and at the time he had not paid any attention to what Lloyd looked like. Then, when everything started happening so fast, he'd left without looking back.  Now, Quinn wasn't sure he'd recognize Lloyd even if the guy walked over and bought him a beer. He'd never seen the face of the man in the car, just the back of his head through the glare of the car window.

He slowly turned around to check out the room behind him. There were groups of people sitting at the tables, but none of them reminded him of Lloyd.  Beyond the tables of people were six pool tables, three of which were being used.  He turned back and took another swallow of beer.  He never tasted the beer as he drank.  All he could think about was Lloyd, but he didn't want it to seem obvious that he was looking for someone.  He waited a few minutes before turning around again and this time looked directly at each player at each table.  Nothing, nobody looked the least bit familiar to him.  He turned back to his beer and took another drink.  Lloyd might not even be in this bar?  He could be at some other business, like next store buying antique furniture, ya, now that sounds like our man.

There was a lot of noise in the bar, music playing, games on TV and people talking and laughing.  But over all the noise and commotion he heard something familiar from a long time ago.  The sound carried across the room and Quinn turned around as soon as he heard it.  "Rack 'em."  That's him, he said to himself.  He glanced quickly over the tables.  There, at the far table on the right, was Lloyd, standing at the end of the table, cue stick in hand.  Quinn turned back to his beer and finished it and set it on the bar, grabbed his hat, got up slowly and started walking back towards the hallway where he came in, glancing over at Lloyd as he went.  Lloyd was busy playing pool, and Quinn was pretty sure he never saw him leave. Confronting Lloyd in a bar when he'd been drinking and was holding a pool stick in his hand, wouldn't have been a smart move.

When he got back to his truck, he climbed in and sat a few minutes thinking of what Emma would say.  "Let's spy on him," he could hear her say, "We'll follow him and see where he goes." Emma loved to play detective, she loved the excitement of investigating a crime and always watched those true life murder shows on television.  This would have been right up her alley.  Not Quinn, this was not his game.  He never liked waiting around for anything, but he thought he might just this once stick around and see what happens.

He decided to move his truck to a better location, somewhere that wasn't so close to Lloyd's car. He drove down to the far end of the parking lot to a spot where he could still see the door of the bar and Lloyd's car. Quinn decided to give Lloyd an hour or so. If nothing happened, he'd leave. He put the seat back to be more comfortable and reached up to pull the sun visors down for a little more concealment. There on the back of the visor was the answer to the one thing that had troubled him. How did Lloyd find him in the first place? It was his auto registration. Lloyd must have seen it at the shop. That's so obvious, why hadn't he thought of it sooner. What else am I missing, he thought, is there something else going on that I'm not aware of? Who is this guy, anyway?

Quinn set his hat on the seat next to him and stretched out and waited. He kept thinking about all the car sightings and why Lloyd always drove away when he came close. He went over it and over it in his head, thinking he was missing something, something important. He closed his eyes trying to picture in his mind everything that had happened. As he sat there almost dreaming about it all he began to get drowsy and slowly he dozed off.

He was awakened abruptly by shouting and screaming and pounding. It was dark outside his truck, but there was Lloyd's face as in a nightmare staring in at him and hammering on the window, yelling at him, "I'm going to kill you. You son of a bitch, you cock-sucking son of a bitch."

Startled, Quinn jumped, started the truck and pulled away as fast as he could. He couldn't believe what had just happened. He was shaking and driving erratically all over the road. When he got to the house, he sped into the driveway and slammed on his brakes, skidding to a stop. He was still shaking when he rushed into the house and locked the door.

Quinn picked up Sugar, grabbed the .38 and went to his bedroom. He sat on the bed, his heart pounding, and tried to think of what to do next. He had to calm down. He set Sugar on the bed and got up and went into the kitchen. He took a glass out of the cupboard, filled it half full with whiskey and walked over to the table and sat down and put the gun on the table in front of him.

"Shit," he said almost shouting, "Lloyd just threatened to kill me." Quinn took a swallow of whiskey and held the glass in front of him with both hands, rolling it back and forth. This was the first time he'd ever been threatened with his life, and he knew this wasn't any joke. Lloyd meant exactly what he said. He was going to kill him if it was the last thing he ever did. Quinn had destroyed this guy's ego in that bar, and that was something he could never let go of. Now Lloyd's the one who doesn't care what happens to him… as long as he gets rid of me, Quinn thought. He knew how anger worked, and it scared the hell out of him.

He knew he had to report this to the police, but he also knew they couldn't do anything on just a threat. At least it would be on the record if anything should happen. After all, Lloyd was an ex-con. With that thought, the panic started to overwhelm him again.

"If I just hadn't fallen asleep, damn it, I'm getting old. I can't even stay awake a few hours to spy," he said feeling like a fool, a foolish old man. He didn't have time to sit around and feel sorry for himself; he had to keep a clear head and think this situation through. Well, at least this old fool found out what Lloyd had planned for him. But how the hell was he going to keep it from happening?

The next day, in the late afternoon, he decided to report the incident to the police and got the response he expected. When he got home, feeling discouraged, he drove clear back to the barn, got out and slammed the door, as angry as he was frustrated. He grabbed a halter in the barn and called out for Bracket. It was getting dark as he saddled his horse. Finally he swung into the saddle, rode out into the street, across the creek and up through the trees to the hills. He then put his heels to his horse and galloped into the night with the lights of the town below and the moon shining bright above. They moved smooth and easy along the crest of the ridge, and he never wanted to stop. Bracket seemed to know his feelings and kept up an even pace that seemed to go on forever. Quinn looked down and watched their moon shadow on the ground as they glided through the night's cool air. Finally he slowed Bracket to a trot and reaching over, patted him on the shoulder, then stopped and just sat looking up into the starlit night. I'll never let that asshole take my life away from me, he thought. He turned Bracket around and they walked slowly back home.

That night, when he was in bed, the slightest sound kept him on edge. He knew that Sugar would alert him if there were an intruder, but it was still hard to sleep, knowing Lloyd was out there somewhere.

The next morning he moved a cot and his sleeping bag into the tack room in the front of the barn. He and Sugar would start spending their nights out there. The tack room had a small window on the wall facing the house. This gave him a view of the backdoor and the driveway all the way to the street. Maybe this would allow him some time advantage should Lloyd decided to break into the house and not find him there.

He also thought that Lloyd might hold off on doing anything for a few days, even a week, to build a false sense of security. But that didn't happen. Sugar and Quinn were in the tack room. Sugar was the first to hear the sound coming from the front of the house and started to growl.

Quinn got right up at the first warning that something was amiss and, slipping into his boots, picked up his cell phone and the gun that was under his pillow. He stood up slowly and looked out the window. It was quiet now, just the wind blowing through the trees. It had rained earlier in the evening, but the clouds were breaking up. A full moon was lighting up the house and yard. He could see the back door and all the way to the street. He heard no unusual sounds, yet he knew Lloyd was nearby. He tried to keep Sugar quiet as he called 911 while placing his thumb on the hammer and slowly pulling it back. Then Lloyd appeared, walking out the back door of his house. He moved from the shadow of the tree and into the moonlight.

So this is big bad Lloyd, Quinn thought. He wasn't that big, now that he could see him clearly for the first time. His long brown straggly hair that had hung to his shoulders and across his eyes was now pulled back tight and tied behind his head; in his right hand he held a gun. Quinn was getting pissed now. He felt assaulted by that worthless piece of shit. "How dare he invade my home like that," he said out loud in anger. Lloyd took a few more steps into the yard and looked over at the barn. Quinn set the cell phone down, gave Sugar a pat on her head, and with the .38 in hand, he opened the door of the tack room and stepped outside, pulling the door shut behind him and latching it. He stood there facing Lloyd, no more than a hundred feet away.

"So Lloyd, what the fuck are you doing in my house?" he said a new-found courage and fearlessness in his voice.

"I'll tell you what the fuck I'm doing. I'm going to kill you. Then I'm going to kill that fucking little dog of yours. And when I'm done with you two, I'm going to kill your stupid horse. And all that will be left of him will be dog food." Lloyd said, his face red with fury.

"I just called 911," was all Quinn could come up with in response to Lloyd's violent threats.

Lloyd laughed. "It will all be over before anyone gets here. All they will have is a mess of blood and guts to clean up. Believe me." Then without another word, Lloyd leveled his gun and pulled the trigger. Quinn's knees buckled as the bullet hit him in the thigh. He rolled over into the shadows, up against the barn wall and fired back, wildly missing everything but the side of his house. It was dark in the breezeway of the barn. Quinn scooted back along the wall to the stall door. Lloyd slowly moved forward, laughing and taunting him. He fired again hitting the ground in front of Quinn scattering dirt into his face. Quinn reached up and opened the stall door and dragged himself inside. He shut and held tight to the door, pulling his wounded body to his feet. He raised his arms at Bracket to scurry him out of the stall and into the safety of the corral. He crawled over to the corner and sat and waited. It was pitch black and smelled of damp hay.

He pulled the hammer back on the gun and labored up onto his feet and peeked over the top of the stall. He could see the silhouette of Lloyd standing in the moonlight at the entrance to the barn. He crouched back down, holding the gun out in front of him with both hands. He moved his left hand to his leg. It was hot and felt sticky, and his pants stuck to the bloody leg. He heard Sugar growl and then she started to bark. "No, Sugar, don't bark." Quinn pulled himself up again and looked down the barn towards the tack room.

The door was open. He couldn't see Lloyd. Then he heard Sugar yelping in pain and Lloyd stepped out of the doorway, holding Sugar up in the air by her tail laughing. "Come and get your little doggie." Quinn hurled himself out of the stall and with uncontrollable anger, he fired his gun, cocked it and rushed off another shot, missing his target, and hurriedly fired again. Then he stumbled and held out his arm to brace himself against the barn wall.

Lloyd pointed his gun at Sugar head and gestured a kiss goodbye. Quinn screamed "NO!" as he hobbled towards Lloyd and fired again, the bullet grazing Lloyd's arm. Tossing Sugar to the side, Lloyd kept laughing and fired back, hitting Quinn in the gut, knocking him backwards onto the ground. Quinn pointed his gun up at Lloyd, but he was getting dizzy, everything was all muddled and hazy. His arm felt weak, like he was holding a hundred-pound weight in the hand. Lloyd slowly walked up and stood over him, looking down on the old man lying there on the ground covered in blood. He started to chuckle. "Damn, I feel good." He laughed loudly as he pointed his gun down at Quinn's head. Then there was the deafening sound of a gun blast, and everything went black.

# CHAPTER TWELVE

There were tears in the corners of his eyes as he kept trying to open them. His eyelids felt heavy, or maybe they were stitched shut. The harder he tried to open them, the tighter they seemed to get. In the far distance, he thought he heard a voice. "Dad, can you hear me? Open your eyes, Dad."

It felt like his body was entangled in tubes of all sizes going in all directions. A large tube seemed to be stuck up his nostril and taped to his face, and another went into the side of his neck, and there were tubes in his arms and in his stomach. Who was doing this to him?

But there was that soft voice again. "Open your eyes."

He moaned, "I'm trying… I'm really trying." His body ached all over with so much pain he thought why not be dead, it would have to be better than this.

"Dad?" It sounded like Anna's voice. Again it spoke. "Dad, can you hear me? Try and open your eyes."

He was struggling to see, but it seemed to take all the strength he had.

"That's good Dad, you're doing good. Can you see me?" Quinn blinked a few times and opened his eyes to just a squint.

"It's me, Dad. You're going to be okay now. We've been really worried about you."

With great effort, he managed to slur, "What happened?" from his dry mouth.

"Don't you remember?"

Remember? He could barely think. "No…. where am I?"

"You're in a hospital."

Quinn had never liked hospitals. Now he knew why "Oh….shit, a hos…pital."

"Yes, a hospital. You've been here for five days."

Days? All he knew right then was it hurts.

"I know, Dad. They're trying to keep you as comfortable as possible."

Comfortable? Quinn closed his eyes again.

"Dad....Dad..."

"Yeah, I'm here." He tried to breathe in some air to speak, but that hurt even more. "What happened?" he whispered.

"You were shot, but you're going to be okay. You're going to be fine."

"Shot?" It sure as hell felt like he'd been shot, but... "How did I get shot?"

"A man came to your house and shot you out in the yard."

"I don't ...I don't know..." He was having a hard time putting words together. He wasn't thinking straight and didn't care; he just hurt.

"Then you shot the man. Do you remember that?"

"No."

Quinn's mind was racing, all the parts floating around in his head, and he couldn't seem to put them in the right places. He was also getting tired and wanted to go back to sleep. "I'm so tired," he said, and with that, he was asleep again.

As he slept, he dreamt he heard that soft sweet voice again. "I love you, Dad." Then strangely it added, "I guess it was too much too soon. We'll have to take it slower." Anna whispered, "I love you Dad." as the voice drifted from the room.

Two days later, Quinn's other daughter, Jessica, was sitting in the chair next to his bed. She had arrived from New York earlier in the week and had seen her dad for only a short time while he was sleeping. Jessica was a sweet girl, always aware of people's feelings. She looked a lot like her mother. She sat next to him, holding his hand and trying not to cry.

Quinn opened his eyes a little and watched her for a bit, just enjoying that he was alive and she was there, before asking, "What's the matter, sweetheart, are you crying?"

"Dad, you're awake. How are you feeling?"

"I don't know; I'm sure I've felt better."

"Do you remember anything about what happened?"

Quinn paused, trying yet again to remember something of that lost night and the sequence of events as he could manage.

"Anna said I shot someone."

"Yes, you shot the man who shot you."

"I remember a man with a gun but that's all." Again he tried to remember more. "You say I shot him."

"Yes, and it was quite a shot at that."

"What?"

"It was an incredible shot, Dad. The police said they've never seen anything…" A knock at the door interrupted them and Quinn's brother looked in. "Come on in, Uncle Will. I was just telling Dad about the shot he made. Maybe you can explain it better." She leaned over and kissed him on his forehead. "I'm glad you're awake and talking, Dad, but you shouldn't overdo it. I'll step out and see you later. I love you."

"So, big brother, what kind of a mess did you get yourself into this time?" Will asked jokingly, a concerned smile on his face.

As Jessica had probably suspected, Quinn felt more comfortable talking with Will about the shooting. "Well, from what I hear, I killed someone."

"That you did brother, that you did. You shot him dead."

Quinn could not help noticing how pleased his brother sounded. "So? Tell me what happened."

"I'll tell you what I know. This Lloyd guy shot you in the gut, and you went over on your back. He must have been standing over you when you shot him. From what I'm hearing, your bullet went right through his open mouth and out the back of his head. It didn't even touch his teeth. That was some shot."

Quinn closed his eyes, trying to imagine what Will had described, then shook his head. "That doesn't sound like me. I'm an awful shot, you know that." Quinn started coughing and Will gave him some water. "The only one I know who could shoot like that was Emma." I guess Emma is still looking out for me, Quinn thought. Maybe she's not quite ready for my arrival.

"You're right, Emma was a damn good shot wasn't she? You think maybe she was holding your hand and aiming the gun for you?"

Quinn smiled weakly and exchanged a look with his brother.

"Anyway," Will said, "Kim is here, and she needs to talk to you. She sent me in to see if you're feeling up to it."

"I don't know how much talking I can do."

"She's here in the waiting room. You don't have to do this now if you're not up to it." For the first time, Will looked at his older brother as if he were an old man who was just barely holding onto life. "Should I go get her?"

Quinn, not wanting to be that old man he saw in his brother's face, pulled what strength he had together and smiled. "Sure, have her come in. This is making me feel real important."

Will laughed and said, "Well, I guess you are important."

After Will left the room, Quinn closed his eyes and went back to sleep. Kim knocked lightly at the door, then opened it and walked in and sat in the chair next to the bed, with her hands folded in her lap, and sat there with sadness on her face, not wanting to disturb him, then got up and started for the door.

"Kim? I'm sorry." Quinn had stirred awake. "I must have dozed off again. Come back please and sit down." He started to cough again, and Kim stood up and held his water so he could sip it through the straw.

"Quinn, do you feel up to talking? I would like to ask you some questions, if you're feeling up to it."

"I'll see how I do," Quinn said, suddenly aware that Kim was there as his lawyer and not his wife's best friend.

"The police want to talk to you. I told them I had to talk to you first."

"The police...?"

"Yes, it's about the shooting the other night. Do you remember the shooting?"

"Oh, yeah, I killed someone, didn't I?" Quinn still could not remember what had happened, but he was starting to get nervous. "I'd told the police that he had threatened to kill me. He shot me first, didn't he?"

"Quinn, it's okay. Everything is going to be fine."

"I told them. I told them he was out there." Quinn was beginning to remember all that had happened before that night and feeling how alone and frightened he'd been.

"I know, Quinn, that's what they want to talk to you about."

"What?" Quinn asked, looking truly confused.

"They want to know why he wanted to kill you."

"Oh... well... that's a long story." Oh, shit, Quinn thought, no one knows about the bar incident. He'd never told anyone, and now it would all have to come out. Even that girl! He didn't want this to happen. How could he get around this?

"I'm your lawyer, Quinn, so you're going to have to tell me everything. Don't leave anything out. Okay? Remember, Quinn, whatever you tell me is just between you and me. It will never go any further. I'm here to give legal advice and moral support."

Kim, Emma's best friend, was not the confessor Quinn would have chosen, but she was good at what she did, so he took a deep breath, had another drink of water, then said, "Do you remember about eight months ago when I went to open the cabin and my truck broke down?"

"Yes, go on." He told her the story about being in the bar and the young girl playing with Sugar and about how the fight had started and ended. But he said nothing about the night in the motel room; he didn't think that it had anything to do with what had happened and he wasn't about ready to try to explain it either.

"Did anyone see Lloyd try to kill your dog?"

"Sure, the girl, his buddies and the bartender, they all saw him."

"Do you know where they are now?"

"No, I don't know." He remembered Titlead's attack that had ended with their car in the ditch. "I haven't seen any of them since that night."

"How did Lloyd find you?"

"He worked at the auto shop that fixed my truck. He must have gotten my address off my registration." Quinn paused and took some deep breaths. He was breathing heavily, and he needed to rest. "Kim, I'm getting tired. Can we do this some other time? I need to rest."

"Sure, I'm sorry, Quinn, you go ahead and sleep. I have all I need for now. I'll come by tomorrow just to see how you're doing, and I'll be with you when the police interview you."

Quinn didn't answer; he was already half asleep. Kim got up and walked to the door, then looked back at Quinn with all the tubes hooked up to him and the machines making their constant noise. How could anyone sleep like that? She shut his door and walked back down the corridor to the waiting room.

It must have been late at night or early in the morning when Quinn heard voices outside his door. He turned his head slightly to the side to listen but quickly closed his eyes as Anna opened the door to look in on him. She stood in the half-open doorway talking to someone in the hallway that sounded like Kim. Anna pulled the door almost completely shut before she spoke again. Quinn could still hear their words, though they were muffled now.

"During his recovery, after he gets out of the ICU, they want to place him in a convalescent home," Kim was explaining to Anna. "He could be there three months or more, depending on any complications. Infections evidently are a big risk. He'll need round-the-clock monitoring."

Anna evidently did not like the idea and raised her voice so that Quinn could clearly hear her say, "No! We can't do that to him! You know how he is... He'd die in a place like that."

Quinn's eyes were wide open now straining to hear every word. Die. How bad off am I? He glanced down at his crippled body, his leg and stomach wrapped in bandages with drains, the IV in his arm, the bags of drip hanging from the stand behind him, the oxygen tubs in his nose, and that constant growling sound of the monitor that set off beeping sounds when it was time to change bags. Yes, it sure looked like he was in a shit load of trouble.

"He should be home, I know it," Anna said as she turned and peeked in the door to make sure he was sleeping. "But we have no way of taking care of him at home. We can't afford full-time nursing, the insurance won't cover it." Then the door was suddenly pulled completely shut, and he could hear no more.

Quinn lay back and stared up into the darkness of his room, wondering what else was going on that he didn't know about. "They're never going to tell me anything they don't think I should know," he said to himself. "They're all just pussy-footing around with my life right now," he whispered, knowing there was not a heck of a lot he could do about it.

Jessica stood quietly by his bed as he slept, looking down at him with tears floating in her eyes, trying her best not to cry. She was glad to see they had removed that awful tube from his nose and that his color seemed much better.

"Hello, Jess." Her father said without opening his eyes.

"How did you know I was here? I was being so quiet."

"I could feel your peaceful calm."

"Thanks, Dad, that's nice." She glanced over at the door then back to her father. "Dad, there's a young girl here that wants to see you."

"A young girl? Who is it?"

"Her name is Jodi.  She says you know her.  She's been here almost every day, sitting out in the waiting room.  She asked if she could come in to visit with you.  Who is this Jodi, Dad?  I've never seen her before, but she seems to think you know her."

"Jodi?"  Quinn said the name out loud a few times, trying to think.  "Jodi?"

"She said you would remember, from your trip to the mountains."

Opening his eyes he glanced towards the door.  "Oh, Jodi…She's here?"

"Yes, she's in waiting room."

"Yes, sure.  I'd like to see her."

"Well, they only let family in."

"Then tell them she's family."

"But Dad, who is she?"

"I'll tell you later.  See if you can get her in, okay."

"All right, I'll see what I can do, but we'd all like to know what's going on."

"I know.  Don't worry.  I'll fill you in later."

After Jessica left the room, Quinn pushed the button on the bed so he could sit up a little.  He didn't want it to look like his injuries were as bad as they were.

Jodi tapped lightly, then, opening the door to his room, stood in the doorway, afraid to move, and looked at him trying not to cry.  She had not expected to see him looking so frail and old and in so much pain.  He was half the man she remembered.  She smiled sadly at him and tried not to look as scared as she was.  She didn't know what to say.  She didn't even know if he'd remember her or that night in his motel room and the money for the bus ticket.  She was more than scared and began to doubt herself and why she was even there.  Quinn could see her apprehension as she stood in the doorway, hesitant to walk in.  "They told me your name is Quinn," she finally said.  "Are you going to be all right?"

"Jodi, come in, come in, sit here.  I'm really glad to see you.  I can see your being good to yourself.  You look wonderful."  Jodi's hair was full and longer now, the piercings were gone and she was even wearing a little makeup.  Her eyes seemed larger and had a glow about them.  She wore a pair of faded jeans and a black parka with an artificial fur-lined hood.  When she finally came in, she moved across the room with a confidence he hadn't seen before.

"Thank you. I heard on television what happened. I'm so sorry. I had no idea he would come after you."

"I know, it's not your fault." Quinn wanted to change the subject. He didn't like talking about Lloyd and what happened to him. He wanted to know about her and her new life now that she had gotten out of that town and away from those people. "So tell me, Jodi, what have you been doing?"

She didn't answer right away. Her eyes kept darting around, trying to take in this scene in front of her. "Are you going to be all right? I need to know."

"Sure, I'll be fine. These doctors really know how to slice and dissect, and they'll have me up and back to normal before you know it. Now, what's going on in your life?"

"Don't be fooling with me, I need to know for real."

"Honest, Jodi, I'm going to be fine, it will just take a little time, that's all."

"I feel sick about what happened, I'm so sorry. I'm so sorry." And she looked down and put her hands to her face and wept.

"It's not your fault and it never was, you're the only bright thing to come from all this. So now, it's only fair that you tell me what your life is like. I need to know that."

"Okay... I'll try." She sniffled and whipped her eyes with a tissue. "When you left that morning, I found the note and the money you left me. I couldn't believe it. You didn't even know me, and yet you did this for me. Nobody had ever done anything like that for me before. So how could I not try? Try to do something, anything... Do you know what I mean?" She shook her hands nervously. "I can't explain it."

"Yes, Jodi, I know what you mean." His mouth was dry, and he took a swallow of water. Her story, like the water, seemed to quench something dry inside him. He had no idea that the little he'd done had meant so much to her.

"I called my cousin, and she said I could come and stay with her in Carson. That's where I live now, with Lori. She's ten years older than me and we get along fine. I've been working in a nice restaurant as a food server, and I'm going to night school studying to be a nurse." She wanted the restaurant to sound like a high-class establishment to impress him with how well she had done. But in reality it was a small coffee shop with older and repeat customers.

"That's great. I knew you could do it." Now that was a lie. He just said it to help build up the new-found confidence he saw in her for the first time. The fact was, he didn't know anything about this girl and hadn't thought once about her since he left that motel. She could have taken the money and gone right back to Lloyd, and he'd have never been the wiser. Nor was he sure that he'd have cared. But she hadn't, and that impressed him right off. "I see you're getting your teeth fixed too."

"Yes, they look pretty silly, don't they?"

"No, not at all, they're going to look real nice."

"The nursing school set me up with the dental school. They're using me as a guinea pig for the students." They both laughed as she smiled real big and tilted her head to show them off.

"I'm so proud of you, Jodi. Look at how much you've accomplished."

"It's because of you. I can never thank you enough."

"No thanks necessary. I'm just glad to see you."

"They won't let me stay long, but can I come back and see you?"

"Sure, I wish you would."

"Here's my phone number." Jodi poked around in her jacket pocket and pulled out a matchbook from the coffee shop where she worked, opened it and with a pen that was sitting on Quinn's bed tray scratched her phone number on the inside cover. "I want you to call me if you ever need anything, okay? I mean it, you call me."

"Okay, thanks." She started to leave her number on his tray. "Don't leave it there. Someone will just throw it away. In that cabinet over there, I think you'll find my clothes, put it in there." Jodi went over and opened the cabinet.

"There's nothing in here… but a pair of boots."

"Put it in one of my boots. They must have got rid of my… dirty clothes."

Jodi closed the matchbook and dropped it into one of the boots and came back to his bed.

"I have to go now, Quinn, but I'll be back."

"You promise, now?"

"I promise." Jodi reached over took hold of his hand. It felt cold. She rubbed it gently, then set it back down and covered it with his blanket and smiled, then turned slowly and walked out of the room.

It would be a long week before Jodi was able to get back to the hospital to see Quinn. By then they had moved him out of the ICU into a room shared with another patient. When Jodi walked in she could see, through an open space in the curtain that separated the two beds, Anna sitting in a chair next to Quinn's bed. She started to leave, when she heard her name called. Anna had spotted her and pulled back the curtain.

"Jodi, don't leave, I'm sure Dad would like to see you," Anna said, just the slightest whiff of sarcasm in her voice.

Jodi hesitated for an instant, then looked directly at Anna and walked over to the foot of Quinn's bed. "I just stopped by to see how your father was feeling."

"I'm glad you stopped by, Jodi, I'm feeling pretty good today," Quinn said.

"I have to go, Dad, and pick up the kids. I'll call you later."

"Okay, honey, I'll talk to you then." Anna nodded at Jodi, picked up her coat and left, leaving behind an uncomfortable void in the room.

"I'm sorry, Quinn, but your daughter Anna does not like me. Maybe I should just stay away and stop coming around to see you."

"Jodi, you've got her all wrong. It hasn't been that long since her mother died, and now she's worried that she's losing her father. Anna's scared. She has too much on her plate right now and too many tough decision to make. It's not that she doesn't like you; she doesn't know you, and right now she doesn't trust anybody, especially when it comes to the care of her father."

"I'm sorry. But I don't want to be a problem to your family."

"Look Jodi. You're not a problem. I'll tell Anna you're my friend."

"I am your friend. When I heard Anna and Kim say they need someone to take care of you, I told them I could do it. But none of them seemed the least bit interested. But they're wrong, I could do it. I have the training and the knowledge to do it." Jodi stood up and turned her back, then walked to the other side of his bed, looking down at him, and confessed, "I understand why they feel this way. I'm not part of your family. I'm an outsider... No, worse than that. I'm the one who caused all this heartache."

"Don't talk like that, I told you it's not your fault."

"I know…but they're right, if it hadn't been for me, none of this would ever have happened." Quinn, perhaps feeling uneasy at her high-strung insistence, started moving nervously in his bed.

"You see! I'm just making thing worse."

"You're not making things worse."

Jodi was about to say something when the curtain was pulled back. She quickly turned around and standing in front of her was the doctor and a nurse. The doctor went up to Quinn, took his hand and put his other hand on his forehead, "How do you feel today, Quinn?"

"Not bad, but I've felt better."

The nurse, who was standing on the other side of the bed looked over at Jodi and said, "We're going to change his dressings now. You'll have to step outside until we're done."

Jodi started to leave, then stopped at the door and turned back toward Quinn as if she had one last word to say. But she didn't speak; she simply smiled and waved goodbye

# CHAPTER THIRTEEN

It was cold in the early morning, on that last day in the hospital. The sky was a dark gray, and it was snowing when they woke Quinn to transfer him to the rehabilitation center. Against their better judgment, the family had decided to put Quinn in the Sparrow Hills convalescent home, where he could get twenty-four hour care while he recovered. None of them wanted to see this happen, but they could find no other option.

Quinn knew how it bothered his family and that they felt ashamed that it had come to this. Putting him in a place like that was the last thing any of them wanted, so Quinn stayed silent and went along peacefully. It was his problem and not theirs, and he didn't want to be a burden or disrupt their lives. He'd gotten into this dilemma all by himself, so he sure as hell could see it through to the end, by himself. His stay at the convalescent home might last as long as eight or ten weeks, and even though he felt good about letting his family off the hook, to Quinn it sounded much like a death sentence.

Anna walked alongside as they wheeled him out to the ambulance. She'd ride inside with her father and Robert would follow along in their car. They rode in silence, Anna was holding her father's hand and feeling overwhelmed with guilt at what was about to become his home for some time. She was afraid it would seem to him like a lifetime. They turned off the highway onto a narrow, heavily wooded road that wound its way alongside the river for another two miles until they came to a large, isolated house set far back off the road. The driver turned into a long driveway and drove around a spacious lawn that was now covered in fresh white snow, to park in front of the main entrance.

Sparrow Hills was an old 1930s Victorian house painted dark lavender with white shutters and trim. Through the gray light of the morning, it looked to be haunted. It was surrounded on all sides by flat, dormant fields with no sign of either sparrows or hills. No one appeared to be about; it seemed deserted, with only the dim glow of faint yellow light coming through the shades of the two front windows. A long veranda stretched across the entire front of the house and around to the sides.

Quinn watched his daughter as they came to a stop. Her body seemed to twitch as if she suddenly woke out of a faraway dream. The attendants got out and moved around to the back and opened the double doors of the ambulance and slid the gurney out with Quinn's frail body strapped on top. They dropped the wheels down and wheeled him up a wooden ramp onto the porch and over to the front door. There were chairs set out on the wooden deck of the veranda, but they sat empty as the cold wind blew through the trees and across the deck, moving the rockers as if spirits from the past had never left. The deck was wet with snow, and the thick paint on the porch railings was cracked and chipped in places.

Quinn held tight to Anna's hand with his eyes shut. A tall, slender woman opened the door and welcomed them in. Anna followed them down the hallway to his room. She tried not to look but still saw the old tired gray shells that once were living, productive people, and their hollow eyes now watching as she passed by.

Quinn was glad when Anna and Robert finally left and he was alone. It was hard for him to look into their faces and see the sadness they felt. He didn't want them to just stand around, trying to think of something to say when there was nothing to be said. This was the way it was going to be, and they all had to get used to it.

Quinn spent hours lying on his back, looking up at the tiny holes in the ceiling tiles. Sometimes he'd start to count the holes in the tiles, then lose his place and have to start all over. But most of the time he'd dream and drift back through his long life, remembering days spent with Emma. It seemed strange to him that he lived through the shooting. He should have been killed, then he'd be with Emma where he belonged, not in a place like this, lying on his back, barely able to move. He thought his life was over. He should just let go and let it end here and now, but something inside him was still fighting to hang on.

From the window in his room he could look out and through the trees and see the white gleam of the river as it flowed south, and with it, the hope that he'd stand, rod and reel in hand, and lay his line upon it.

Every day he tried time and again to sit up and move his body through the pain, only to fall back, exhausted. On the fifth day, he was able to sit up and hang his feet over the side of the bed. Three days later, he put his feet on the floor to try to stand, but the pain put him flat on his back. For the next two days, he did nothing.

On Sunday, Quinn sat watching a football game on television, only to fall asleep during the fourth quarter. He slept for about an hour and awoke to the sound of an old familiar voice. The game had ended, and the National Finals Rodeo from Las Vegas was on. Some commentator was interviewing an old cowboy, who was telling stories of the old days of rodeo back in the late 50s and 60s. "So Deek, what ever happened to your partner, Quinn Adams? Do you two ever get together and talk about the old days?"

"Tell you the truth, I haven't seen nor talked with him in oh, maybe six years. His wife had cancer and passed on, and now I heard he was in the hospital from gunshot wounds. Seems he got involved in an ol'-fashioned Western shootout."

"Yes, I remember seeing that on the news. That was really something."

"I thought I'd stop by and see him on my way back to Montana."

"Tell the folks how you two first met."

"It was during a rodeo in Billings Montana in 58. Neither of us had a dime between us. Quinn swiped a bottle of ketchup off a table in a saloon, and we made tomato soup out of it for supper that night, and it got us through 'til the next day's events, where we made a little money."

Quinn sat and listened to Deek's bullshit and swore at the television. "He's a damn liar. That never happened." Quinn remembered an old black cowboy telling them that story in a bar in Pendleton, Oregon and now Deek is using it as part of his repertoire.

Quinn often wondered why Deek never called or came by to visit after Emma became ill with her cancer. He thought it must have scared him to see someone like Emma going through what she had to endure. He probably didn't know what to say or how he'd react. I guess a lot of people get scared off when someone comes down with a terminal disease. It must just be human nature. Maybe they think it's contagious.

Days slipped by, and he knew he was sliding into depression. He had to start doing something to help himself. Stretched out on his back, he made tight fists with his hands and tightened his arms and then relaxed them. Then he'd do it again and again, over and over, tighten and relax, tighten and relax. Then he'd do the same thing with his legs, repeating it several times a day, keeping count, trying always to do just one more then the last time. Slowly he started to build up his strength. By the end of the third week he managed to make it to the bathroom by holding on to the wall and inching along, shuffling his feet little by little until he reached the bathroom, where he collapsed onto the toilet. He was in excruciating pain and physically exhausted. He felt light-headed and thought he might pass out. He wavered back and forth on the toilet and tried to stand, but he couldn't. He had to call for help to get back to his bed, but he never stopped trying, and when the pain got bad, he'd put it out of his mind by thinking about something else, like eating ice cream.

After two more weeks, Quinn was able to make it to the bathroom and back to his bed on his own, still using the wall for support. On one of his trips back from the bathroom, he started to lose his balance as he approached his bed and had to brace himself up against a cabinet. He steadied himself by holding on to the cabinet door, but it swung open, and he fell to the floor. He sat there, looking into the open cabinet. There inside, his clean clothes hung on hangers and on the floor sat his boots. He looked up at what seemed to be his only connection to what had been his real life.

All he wanted now was to get up, put his clothes on and get the hell out of there. He was so tired of being in bed and in those stupid open gowns they made him wear, that he had almost forgotten what it was like to be dressed in real clothes, like a real person. He hadn't worn his jeans in a long time, and sitting on the floor looking at his clothes brought back old memories. Memories of the mountains and streams with Sugar and Bracket and longing for the days spent together in the cold, clean, fresh air of the mountains. As hard as that trip had been, it sure as hell was a damn sight better than being a prisoner in Sparrow Hills.

Quinn started again to get up on his feet. He began pulling himself up by holding on to the cabinet door but slipped off and fell, knocking over one of his boots. Trying once more, this time bracing himself against the cabinet and holding onto the door, he finally made it to his feet. He stood there, out of breath, wobbling and little dizzy, remembering when standing up was not his most impressive accomplishment of the day. Putting out his hand to steady himself, he bent over to put his boot back in the cabinet. He blinked as something caught his eye. Reaching inside the boot, he pulled out a matchbook and opened it. Written on the inside cover were numbers. He read them one by one out loud. He'd forgotten all about it. That seemed so long ago. He said the numbers over and over as if he was afraid of losing them again and they'd disappear forever.

Back in his bed, he lay there on his back to rest, the matchbook held tightly in his hand. He raised up his hand and read it one more time, then let his arm fall to his side and shut his eyes and slept.

Two hours later, the attendants came into his room with dinner. They set it on the tray in front of him, saying nothing, and walked out, shutting the door behind them. Quinn woke up and pushed the button to raise the bed up into a sitting position.

The meal smelled of old frozen food that had been sitting out too long. He was still on a soft food diet and hated everything, no matter what it was. As he opened his hand to take his spoon, the matchbook fell onto the bed beside him. He set his spoon back on the tray and picked it up, then reached over for the phone.

"Jodi?"

"No, this is Lorie."

"Oh, I'm sorry, I must have the wrong number."

"No, wait, you have the right number. I'm Jodi's cousin. Just a minute and I'll get her."

Quinn could hear Lorie's muffled voice in the distance then what sounded like a brief shriek then more muffled conversation. He was beginning to wonder if he had made a mistake by calling when he heard a low nervous voice ask, "Quinn?"

"Yeah, hi, Jodi, how are you?"

"I'm fine now, but I've been miserable, I thought I would never hear from you again. Thank you for calling. How are you? Where are you?" For some reason Quinn found himself reminded of high school.

"Hold up, one thing at a time."

"I couldn't find you." Jodi said. "I went back to the hospital and you were gone. No one would tell me where you were."

"Well, I'm right here."

"And where exactly is right here?" Jodi said with a childlike giggle. She was still so nervous to be talking to him. It sounded like she was meeting a rock star for the first time. "Tell me how you're doing."

"I'm getting better. I should live, if the food doesn't kill me."

"Oh, I'm glad. I'm so glad you're doing better."

"This place smells funny. I hate it in here."

"Now listen, Quinn, tell me your phone number and the name of the place where you're staying. I want to come and see you."

"I'd like to see you, too. I couldn't call any sooner because I forgot where your number was until just a few minutes ago. I knocked over my boot and there you were, right here all the time."

Quinn told Jodi all she needed to find him. He also told her where his house was and how she could get inside and find the keys to his truck, just in case she needed a vehicle. There was a long pause as if Jodi were catching her breath, then she asked, "Will they let me in to see you?"

"Sure, why not? I'm not in jail, although sometimes it feels like it. If they give you any trouble, just tell them you're my daughter."

"Quinn, come on, daughter? How about, I'm your granddaughter. That might be more believable. Besides, they've already met your daughters."

"Okay, I guess you're right, granddaughter. That's just going to make me feel older, you know that don't you?" After an awkward silence, he asked, "When do you think you'll be able to come by?"

"Just a minute."

Quinn could hear their muffled voices in the background, then Jodi said, "We'll be there in about an hour."

"Not til then, eh?"

"Is that okay?"

"That'll be fine, I ain't going nowhere. You drive safely, now."

Quinn lay back in his bed and smiled up at the ceiling tiles. An hour and twelve minutes later according to the digital clock on his TV's cable box, there was a light knock on his door, then it slowly opened. Jodi stood in the door way, and in her arms she held a small bouquet of flowers and on her face was a shy grin.

"Come on in, welcome to my world," Quinn said from his bed.

"Quinn, I made it." She rushed over to him and hugged him.

"I'm so glad you came. I've missed you. Here, get that chair and move it over here. Sit down. I want to hear about all you've been doing." Seeing Jodi again boosted his spirits. He felt like rushing out and showing her his real life. But he couldn't even walk across the room without help. They sat and talked for what seemed like hours, but it had only been about twenty minutes, when Quinn asked Jodi, "Will you help me break out of here and get back to my house?"

"Sure, if that's what you want. I'll do whatever I can."

"You would have to sneak me out. I don't think they'll let me just get up and go without signing a lot of papers and calling the doctors and my daughters"

"You really are a prisoner."

"Afraid so."

"Tell me what you want me to do."

"Is your cousin here with you?'

"Yes. She's out in her car waiting for me. She's parked at the curb."

"How would she feel about helping out?"

"Are you kidding? She will love the excitement of a breakout."

"Will we all fit in her car?"

"Sure, she has a four door and there's lots of room."

"Are you sure you don't mind doing this? I don't want you girls to get in any trouble or anything."

"No one is going to get in trouble. Remember, you're not really in jail, you can come and go as you wish, and we're just going for a ride, right?"

"You're right, we're just going for a ride." Quinn still wasn't sure about getting the girls involved, but he wanted so much to get out of there that he'd try almost anything.

"Jodi." He looked down at his legs for a second, then said, "You know I can't walk, I want you to know that. I can just barely get to the bathroom by hanging on to the wall, and sometime I need help getting back to my bed."

"We'll be alright. I'll help you. I had a whole class on care for the infirm. Piece of cake."

"No, Jodi. Listen to me, you don't understand. If we get me home, you'll have to stay there and help me until I can help myself, and that could be weeks. Do you hear what I'm saying? It could be weeks. You won't be able to leave. I need help day and night."

"I'm okay with that. I want to stay and help you."

"Jodi, you have a job and school. You have to think about that, it's not going to be easy for you."

"I just finished a semester, so I can pick up school at any time. As far as my job goes, the people would completely understand. They like me and would give me back my job whenever I asked. I'm sure of that."

Quinn didn't want to put her on the spot like this, but he knew he was taking advantage of the girl. He was being selfish and he hated himself for it, but he couldn't see any other way out. I'll make it up to her somehow, he told himself, but right then he needed her help.

"All right Jodi, this is what I want you to do. Go out to the front desk and ask if you can use a wheelchair to take me for a walk around outside, to get some fresh air and sun light."

"Okay, I'll be right back. Don't go anywhere while I'm gone." Jodi chuckled, enjoying her little joke.

Quinn raised his head with a grin. "Oh, I'll be right here waiting."

When Jodi walked out of the room to find a wheelchair, he sat on the edge of his bed and tried to dress himself. He had to do it in small steps and then rest to catch his breath. As he rested, he looked around the small little room he had been in for what seemed like a lifetime. He'd spent most of the time in the room alone with only his thoughts. As he buttoned his shirt he thought of Anna, she came by almost daily, but she never had time to stay long. She had to pick up the kids or had things to do before Robert got home. He understood, their lives were busy; they had things to do. As he tried to pull on his pants while sitting on the edge of the bed, he kept reminding himself that that was what he wanted: a busy life with things to do.

At night it was hard to sleep. His mind kept thumbing through his life like quick snap shots. Being alone and confined he'd try to relive the times he and Emma spent together. He still missed her so and longed to hold her in his arms again and have her by his side and smell her sweetness and share his thoughts and ideas with her. When the pain got bad he would think of holding her hand and looking at her beautiful smiling face. Her smile alone could make the pain go away.

When Jodi returned with the wheelchair, Quinn pretty much had his clothes on, and she helped him with his boots.

"Did you have any trouble?"

"No, they were very helpful," Jodi said. "There weren't any wheelchairs out front, so they sent someone to go get one for me. The lady at the desk thought it was sweet of me, your granddaughter, to be taking you out for a walk. She said I was a lovely young lady." Jodi smiled a big smile as she pushed the chair up close to Quinn's bed and set the brake.

"She's right. You are a lovely young lady." Quinn slid into the chair. Jodi released the brake and pushed him out of the room and down the hall to the front door. The lady at the desk came over and held the door open for them. They thanked her and went outside, down the ramp to the sidewalk and over to Lorie's car. Lorie saw them coming and rolled down her window as they approached her car.

"Lorie, I would like you to meet Mr. Adams." Jodi said, "We're going to take him for a little ride, if that is all right with you."

"Sure, I'm glad to meet you, Mr. Adams. Where would you like to go?"

"I thought we might drive over to my house and I'll show you around."

"I'd love that. You get up front with me, there's more room." Lorie said.

They left the wheelchair on the sidewalk and drove off down the driveway to the street and were gone.

# CHAPTER FOURTEEN

Once Sparrow Hills was out of sight, Quinn turned to Lorie and said, "It's mighty nice of you to help with the jail break." And they all burst into laughter.

From the back seat Jodi giggled, "She just held the door open for us and your sweet granddaughter wheeled you right out."

"How long do you think it will take before they realize that you're gone?" Lorie laughed.

"Not till they come by to pick up my dinner dishes and realize I didn't eat that gourmet meal." Quinn could not remember when he had laughed so much, his face hurt from smiling almost as much as his healing wounds ached from laughing. "Say, is there any chance we could stop and get a burger? I can't remember the last time I had any real food."

Lorie pulled into the first drive-in she spotted and Jodi ran in to get a burger and fries. Lorie sat alone with Quinn, the laughter was gone and she turned to him and said.

"Jodi's told me what you did for her."

Quinn shook his head and tried to shrug it off.

"No, Mr. Adams, you changed her life. You saved her. And Jodi knows it." Lorie looked at the uncomfortable expression on Quinn's face. "And you should know it too. You mean the world to her."

At this point Jodi opened the car door, "I got the burger deluxe with cheese, bacon, lettuce, tomato, super... Hey, why is everyone so glum? I even got double fries and onion rings." She handed this mouthwatering feast in its paper bag to Quinn and jumped into the back seat. "Let's get out of here before we're spotted."

Lorie put the pedal to the metal and took off. Jodi scooted up and leaned forward, crossing her arms on the back of the front seat. "I sure hope I'm not going to be sorry for getting you that greasy burger. You'll probably up-chuck it all over Lorie's car and I'll have to clean it up."

Quinn said with a mouth full of food and trying not to laugh at the same time, "It's a great burger Jodi, but keep an eye out the back and make sure we're not being followed."

Then Loric asked, "What if they set up a road block?"

"Run it!" Quinn said, and the laughter began again. They were acting like a bunch of teenagers who were cutting school for the first time and he was enjoying every minute.

Sitting up in the car began to get uncomfortable for Quinn. The pain he had laughed through was returning but he didn't care, he was free and having fun for the first time since he couldn't remember when. The sights and sounds of the road under him and the trees passing by his window all told him he'd never return to that prison cell. He'd die in his own bed first.

Quinn's spirit had come to life but as they turned into his driveway a sadness came over him. The girls got out and left him alone in the car while they went to find the key to the house and make things ready for him. Quinn sat in silence, his eyes taking in the welcome sight of his home. From where he sat, he could see the tack room and the small window he had looked out that terrifying night. He quickly turned back towards the house.

The girls were inside the house now, and he recalled the day he and Anna had brought Emma home from the hospital after her first cancer surgery and helped her up those same steps. Emma was never one to complain but you could see it in her eyes, the awful agony she was going through.

Quinn looked up when he heard Jodi tapping lightly on his window with the tip of her forefinger as if she didn't want to startle him.

"Are you ready?"

Quinn nodded and reached up and unlocked his door then reached across and unclasped his seat belt. Jodi opened his door and he turned in his seat and reached up with his arms. The girls helped him out of the car and onto his feet. He was dizzy and wavered a little, then said, "Okay, let's get this old body in the house."

With his arms around the girls' shoulders they walked him over to the steps. There were four steps up to the front porch deck. Quinn looked at them like it was a mountain to climb. How did Emma ever get up those steps into the house?

He put his hand on the banister and his weight on Jodi and with the help of Lorie the two girls managed to get him up onto the porch and into his room where he gave-out and lay exhausted on his bed. Jodi took his boots off and covered him with a blanket and he dropped off to sleep.

It was dark when Quinn woke with the sound of voices coming from the front room of his house. He propped himself up on his elbows to listen. "Sounds like the posse arrived." Quinn said to himself then lay back down. He could hear Jodi trying to explain to his daughter.

"Anna, I know you're upset with me and I don't blame you one bit… But he's here now and this is where he wants to be."

"You're right, I was furious. Now I've calmed down. I'm going in to see my Dad and then we're going to have a talk." He could hear Anna walking down the hall towards his room and as she came through the doorway he looked up at her with a devilish grin on his face, like a little boy who had just played a trick on his parents.

"Is everyone getting along?"

"Yes Dad, we're all getting along. How do you feel?"

"I feel much better now that I'm home and in my own bed."

"How did you handle the ride over here?"

"We made it fine."

"Dad, I know you belong here…"

He interrupted her. "I do belong here."

"I know Dad. It was just a matter of taking care of you, that's all."

"I'm better now. I'm not in some critical state."

"I know Dad. But is she responsible, can she handle it?"

"I don't know, but I'm willing to give her a chance."

"We don't know anything about her, we don't…"

He interrupted again. "Look, honey, I love you and I know you only want what's best for me. Let's see how this works out and if there are any problems, you'll be the first to know."

"Well, let me go talk to her and see what she wants to do. If you feel comfortable about it, then we'll just see how it works." Quinn could tell that Anna still wasn't convinced but she didn't have much of a choice. She had to let the cards fall where they may. Quinn propped himself back up on his elbows so he could hear better on what was being said in the other room.

Jodi, before Anna had a chance to say anything, began to introduce her cousin to everyone. "Lorie drove us here and has nothing to do with any of this."

"Okay, that's fine." Anna said. "He's resting now, and he looks good. So Jodi, what's next?"

It was quiet at first as if Jodi was trying to think where to begin. She took a deep breath, looked down at the floor then raised her head and began to explain. "I'm going to call my job tomorrow and quit. I just finished my semester finals at the nursing school, so my time will be Quinn's until he is able to take care of himself. Then, I'll go get another job and finish school. But for now I'll live here and take care of what needs to be done. I did some research on Quinn's injury so I know what to look for and how to care for him. If there is something I can't handle or if an emergency should arise I'll call 911 and I'll call you. I had Lorie go to the drugstore to pick up some things I thought we might need right away. Lorie will be going home tonight."

"That's fine. But now... what kind of a fee would you like for your services?" Anna asked.

"Nothing, I don't want any payment."

"Nothing? That's ridiculous. You must want something for all the work you'll be doing."

"I know it's hard to understand. I don't even understand it all myself. But Quinn said some things to me that put my life on the right path, or I would have been lost forever.

"I can't even remember what it was that he said, but it doesn't really matter now because it's done. I don't think Quinn even knows what he said or what he did for me."

"That's interesting but......"

Jodi cut her off and continued on, "I'll try to explain it the best I can. It was like setting off an alarm in my head and my life changed. I get chills when I think about it." Jodi held up her hand as if to prevent them from speaking and went on with her story. "You see I came from a very dysfunctional home. It was bad, bad things were done to me. I didn't even know how bad they were, all I know is, I was lost in a dark place with no way out. Then Quinn with his few hard words of advice entered my life. It was like someone opening a window and letting in fresh air. It must have always been there, hidden deep in my soul because when he spoke to me I could feel it rise up and flow to the surface. Quinn got me out of that dark world and he doesn't even know it."

They were all silent and just staring at her. Quinn, in the other room could hear most of what Jodi was saying but it didn't sound like she was talking about him. He'd never said anything to change anyone's life. And if he'd ever tried, he doubted anyone would have listened. He'd always found that people just don't care much about what other people have to say.

It was quiet now and Quinn had a feeling that Jodi was getting uncomfortable, then she spoke again, "It's all the truth, honest."

"Well that's quite a story, Jodi." Anna said feeling a sadness she wasn't expecting, "I believe you." There was a stillness throughout the room. Everyone seemed to be moved by Jodi's story, even her cousin Lorie who had never heard Jodi tell it like that before. Jodi had told her some of this earlier while driving to the convalescent home but it never hit home like it did now as Jodi stood there in front of everyone baring her soul. She told them all this, not to show her sincerity but to try to make them understand what a special event had happened to her. "I wished you all could have experienced the unbelievable feeling that flowed through me." It became quiet again and Quinn sat up and leaned forward, afraid he was missing something. Then he heard his daughter speak up.

"Jodi, Dad can afford to pay you. You should never work for nothing. It's not fair to you or to us."

"I'm not working for nothing. I have already been paid. I'm just paying back, so to speak." Anna looked over at Robert speechless for the first time, then decided to let it go for now but thought she'd come up with some way to pay Jodi for her time. The evening ended well and they all agreed that Quinn belonged back at home. Jodi had convinced them that she was more than capable of taking care of Quinn at this point in his recovery. He was basically in good health. It was just a matter of time now. Anna and Robert went home feeling better and promised to help Jodi whenever she needed anything.

Jodi walked Lorie out to her car and thanked her again for all her help. Lorie told her she would pick up some of her things and bring them over in a few days.

"I'm going to really miss you." Lorie said.

"I'll miss you too."

As Lorie was getting into her car to leave she stopped and turned to Jodi, "You never mentioned that Quinn was such a good looking man. Do you think that might have something to do with your attraction towards him?"

"Do you think?" Jodi asked.

"Well yeah."

"Go home." Jodi said and they both laughed.

"I'll see you in a few days."

Jodi turned and walked back into the house and shut and locked the door behind her. She stood alone in the middle of the living room. There was restful calm through-out the house now that everyone had left. She was nervous and a little scared. Had she over sold herself? Was she really going to be able to handle all this responsibility? "Yes I'll be fine." She told herself, "It's just a case of nerves on the first day of the job." Jodi went in to check on Quinn before going to her room for the night. Quinn was awake and winked at her with a grin as she walked in.

"Did my daughter give you the old 1-2 punch? And how did you hold up?"

"We all got along fine. I think she is going to be alright with this arrangement."

"Well I know I am." He paused for a second then said, "I overheard some of your conversation…"

"Don't embarrass me, Quinn."

"No, no I would never." And he let it drop.

"Is there anything I can get you?" She asked.

"Yes, you can help me to the bathroom before I call it a night. Okay?"

"Sure, we might as well get started and what better place to start than the toilet."

Quinn beamed, "I think you just might work out after all."

"Tomorrow I'm going to go get you a walker. This holding onto walls is stupid and besides a walker can help you with your balance. All this leaning against the wall is probable throwing your spine out of adjustment."

"I don't want a walker, they're for old people."

Jodi helped Quinn sit up on the edge of the bed, then onto his feet.

"Well, you're getting one anyway. The more you use it the faster you'll get rid of it. It will help you strengthen your muscles in the correct walking position."

She put her arm around his waist and he put his arm on her shoulder.

"Well I can sure see who's in charge. They were a lot nicer at the home."

"Do you want to go back?"

"Hell no."

"Then you're going to have to do as you're told."

They labored their way towards the bathroom, stopping once at the bathroom door so Quinn could steady himself before continuing on.

"Boy, are you strict. Remember I'm a sick old man, where is your compassion?"

"Compassion comes when you do as you're told."

"You know I can fire you."

"No you can't. I haven't been hired."

Jodi turned him around in front of the toilet. "Can you take it from here?"

"Yes ma'am. I have some pajamas in the bottom dresser drawer."

"Alright, you call me when you're done and I'll get you changed."

"I think I can manage by myself."

"Now don't be shy, I am your nurse."

They kept smiling and joking with each other both knowing they were going to get along just fine. The fun and laughter was something neither one of them had had in a long time.

## CHAPTER FIFTEEN

Jodi had taken control over Quinn's life, and Quinn was getting worried that she might be getting too comfortable in her new nursing capacity. Jodi did everything around the house, all the cooking, cleaning, marketing; she even drove Quinn in his truck to and from his doctor's appointments.

She woke Quinn early each morning to start him on his physical therapy. From room to room, up and down the hallway Quinn would maneuver his walker back and forth under Jodi's watchful eyes. She'd push him to go longer and farther each day.

"Okay, okay, that's it." Quinn finally said. "I'm taking a break. Remember, I'm an old wounded soldier."

"You're not a soldier, a soldier wouldn't quit. One more time, down the hallway and back."

Jodi kept pushing him, egging him on. "Cowboy up, Quinn, I want to see some life in your steps."

"I'm not going to take this any longer. I'm calling Anna and telling her how you're mistreating me."

Jodi just laughed, and Quinn sulked back at her.

One morning Quinn lay in bed and refused to get up, said he was taking the day off. Jodi stood at the door to his room, looking down at him. She slowly walked up to his bed, bent over, took hold of his covers and ripped them back. "I have a lot to do today, and I'm not taking the day off and neither are you!"

And as the days went by, Quinn couldn't argue the fact that his condition had continued to improve. Within the second week Quinn had trashed his walker and was now able to move around the house using only a cane for support. Even Anna was impressed with Jodi and how she had taken charge and was taking such great care of her father. She kept offering to put her on some kind of salary, but Jodi would have none of it. As far as Jodi was concerned, like she told them before, she had already been paid.

Quinn's health got better and better. In the third week, Quinn asked his daughter if she would bring Sugar back. He missed her and thought it was time for her to come home.

It was late afternoon and the sun felt warm on Quinn's face as he stepped outside onto the back porch and glanced over at the empty corral. Sugar was coming home and that was good, but Quinn was yearning to get back on his horse and head out into the hills where he could feel the freedom that was missing from his life. He turned and sat against the railing and began to tap his cane nervously on the porch deck. He called out to Jodi, who was in the kitchen doing dishes.

She put the glass she was drying on a shelf in the cupboard and closed it. "Are you all right?" she asked, then walked around to the screen door.

"Yeah, I'm fine. I was just wondering...do you know how to ride a horse?"

"Well, no. But I tried once." She opened the door and stepped outside, "A girl friend and I once climbed through this fence into a pasture. There were a lot of horses out grazing. We ran after them and tried to jump on their backs, but they never stood still long enough, and we always ended up on the ground."

"It sure doesn't sound like you're afraid of horses."

"No, I don't think I am, but I haven't been around them in years, so I really don't know how I'd react."

"We're going to find out."

"What do you mean, find out?" She felt uneasy.

"Tomorrow we're going to hitch up my trailer and go get Bracket."

"Bracket, is that the horse you rode on that trip when I met you?"

"Yeah, that's the one. He's out at my brother's ranch in a pasture. We're going to go get him and bring him back to the house and then I'm going to teach you how to ride. Not being able to ride a horse is un-American."

Jodi knew that Quinn was born and raised on a cattle ranch and that he thought that people took to horses like fish to water. Jodi was never the outdoor adventurous type. To her, riding a horse was sitting in front of a television watching a Western movie. She was not too sure that horseback riding was part of her job requirements. She was again being led in an entirely new and strange direction that had her a little on edge.

"I don't know about riding a horse, that's really not my kind of thing." she said, knowing that it didn't make any difference what she said because Quinn had already made up his mind and she was going to learn how to ride.

The next day Quinn called his brother Will and told him his plan to pick up Bracket. Will said he was doing fine and was just getting fat out in the pasture and needed to be ridden. "Come by the house and I'll ride out with you." Will said.

"I'm bringing Jodi with me. I'm still under my nurse's care, you know."

"Great, I would like to see her. Are you planning to give her riding lessons?"

"Yeah, how did you know that?"

"Just a hunch, but I thought I should warn her about the way you give lessons."

Quinn smirked at his brother's remark. "There's nothing wrong with the way I give lessons."

"Oh, just talk to some of your previous students."

Will, who was always good at judging a man's character, thought that Jodi was as solid as a rock and that the others had misjudged her.

Quinn was feeling especially good this day and he knew it was because he was going to bring his horse home. Everything seemed to be going in the right direction, but he was worried about Jodi. She had been working hard and never complained about anything. He told her to take some time off, a little break, and suggested she go see her cousin for the weekend. Jodi protested at first, saying she was fine and didn't need any time off, but eventually said she would go. Quinn needed his space and didn't want to get tired of her always being there. He thought the separation would be good for both of them. He wasn't used to having someone around twenty-four hours a day since he lost Emma.

In the afternoon, Jodi went out to help Quinn hitch up the trailer. Quinn decided to let Jodi back the truck to the trailer while he stood off to the side and directed her in the alignment of the truck to the trailer hitch.

"All right, Jodi, bring her back slowly, a little to the right, a little more, no, no, too much, go forward again. Now slowly bring her back, cut it to the left, good, a little more, no, no, go forward again."

Jodi was getting nervous, beads of perspiration popping out across her forehead. "One more time, Jodi, we almost have it. Watch my hands when I motion you to stop or turn to the left or right, okay, you ready?"

There was no response from Jodi, she just sat and stared straight ahead, and then the truck door opened and Jodi stepped out and turned and stood facing Quinn. She raised her right hand and wiped her brow, then placing both hands on her hips, looking out of sorts, she said, "No, you do it, I'll direct you." and she walked to the back of the truck.

"All right, that can work." Quinn took his hat off and slapped it against his leg, got in the cab, put his hat on the dash and backed the truck to the trailer, and the two of them headed off for the ranch.

"Wait!" Jodi said, jumping out of the truck and running back into the house. When she came back, she was carrying Sugar in her arms. Anna had brought Sugar to the house earlier in the day but wasn't really sure she wanted to part with her. She had taken Sugar to the Doggie Salon and once again her hair was silky white. Anna had tied a pink bow in Sugar's hair in hopes of convincing her dad that the dog would be out of place around the stables. Quinn had only smiled. "A real man's dog," he said, insisting that Sugar stay. Anna reluctantly turned her over to him.

Jodi set Sugar on the seat between them and closed the door. She also brought along three large carrots just in case they had trouble catching Bracket out in the pasture. She sat quietly holding the carrots on her lap as Quinn drove. He glanced over at her and could tell there was something on her mind.

"What's the matter, Jodi? Is something bothering you?"

"No... I just sometimes get some old feelings coming up. It's nothing, really."

Quinn knew she'd had a troubled childhood and looked back at her with a sympathetic smile.

She gave a quick smile back. "How much further is it?"

"Not much farther, fifteen minutes, maybe."

Quinn pulled up in front of the house and got out. He stood resting his arm on the open door and reached back inside to poke the horn twice. Will came to door, waved and walked up to the truck as he put on his jacket. Jodi opened her door, put Sugar on her lap and slid over to make room. Will sat down next to Jodi and gave her a quick hug. "How's he been treating you, Jodi? He isn't working you too hard, is he?"

"No, he's been real nice to me. We've been getting along great and he's even giving me the weekend off." Jodi forced a big smile.

"Well, big brother, you're getting real soft-hearted in your old age."

"I've always been soft-hearted, you're just never around when it happens."

"You're right about that."

Quinn started the truck and drove forward, turning onto a bumpy, narrow dirt road. He drove about three-quarters of a mile to a long ranch gate that opened up into a ten-acre grass field. There were seven horses standing in the tall grass, grazing. Only one raised his head and looked over in their direction, when they stopped the truck and got out. "He knows the sound of my truck." Quinn said.

Jodi looked over at him, "He can remember the sound of your truck?"

"Horses have a good memory," Will said. "He'll probably walk right up to Quinn, you'll see." And that's exactly what happened. Will got out and unlocked the gate. Quinn reached behind the seat for the halter and stepped around to the front of the truck. Bracket came right up to him and let Quinn slip the halter on and walk him back to the trailer.

Jodi got out with her carrots, broke them in half and fed them to Bracket. "You're going to make me ride him?" She glanced over at Quinn's brother, hoping for a little support.

"That's right. He'll be real good to you, don't you worry." Quinn could tell Jodi was impressed with the size of Bracket as he stood towering over her. She was shaking in her boots right now, wondering, how am I going to climb up on his back?

"What if he doesn't like me?"

"He already likes you. You gave him all those carrots." Will put Bracket in the trailer for Quinn and secured him. "Do you think you'll have any trouble getting him out when you get home?" Will asked.

"No, we'll be fine, thanks for your help." They dropped Will off at his house on their way out. Will's wife and two of their sons came out to say hello, and Quinn introduced them to Jodi. They talked for a few minutes and joked about Quinn's riding instructions, and they all had a good laugh at his expense.

Quinn was watching Jodi as her eyes lit up and held a constant grin on her face. She kept looking from one to another as they all joined in on the teasing.

As Quinn drove off, Jodi turned and glanced back, watching as they went into their house, then looked over at Quinn. "You sure have a nice family."

"Yeah, they're a good bunch."

"I really enjoyed meeting them."

Quinn came to an intersection and stopped and turned to Jodi. "They liked meeting you too." She smiled and sat back with Sugar on her lap and they drove home.

That night after they put Bracket away, Quinn gave his truck keys to Jodi and said, "Tomorrow you take my truck and go see Lorie. Have some fun for a few days, and when you get back, we'll start you with your riding lessons. It will give you a chance to relax and have some time for yourself." The way he said it, it sounded so final. She had no response.

On Quinn's last doctor visit, his doctor had made some changes in his pain medicine, and now Quinn was having trouble sleeping at night. He was having strange dreams, some verging on nightmares. The night Jodi left for the weekend Quinn had another strange dream. He was lying in bed on his back and Emma was lying next to him in his arms, resting her head on his shoulder. He was caressing her hair. It felt soft and silky as they lay there together, eyes shut and drifting off into sleep. As Quinn was stroking Emma's hair the softness turned coarse and into stiff stubbles of hair. Quinn opened his eyes to see, and staring back at him were hollow empty holes. The eye-holes of the gutted deer that had hung from the cabin deck. He jumped, then sat up in bed, ringing wet and in a cold sweat. He thought he had screamed out loud but he wasn't sure if he'd dreamt that, too. Quinn lay awake the rest of the night, afraid the dream would return.

During the day he felt uneasy and couldn't get that horrible image out of his mind. The next night he slept fine, and in the afternoon, when he heard his truck pull into the driveway, his spirits rose and he went to the door to greet her.

Quinn walked out of the house onto the porch with a big smile on his face. He noticed Jodi looked a little uneasy and didn't seem very happy to see him. She got out of the truck and slammed the door and started walking towards him.

"How was your weekend? Did you have a good time?" He knew the answer before she said a word.

"No, I didn't have a good time, thank you." And she started to cry, then stopped and wiped her eyes with the back of her hands. She looked up at him standing on the porch. Her eyes were red and her cheeks moist. "It was a bad idea." She tossed him the keys to the truck and walked right past him to her room, shutting her door.

Quinn stood there speechless as he watched her pass by. He was confused by her sudden behavior. Maybe she realized how confined she's been and was just sick of being stuck here with an old man. Or maybe she'd picked up on his desire for time alone. Whatever it was, he was going to have to give her some time before he said what needed to be said. Women, they're a strange breed, he thought. They all must come from the same bloodline. He went in the house and sat down in his chair and turned on the television and waited.

About thirty minutes later, Jodi came out of her room with her emotions in control and sat down across from Quinn, who was watching a basketball game on ESPN. He reached over and picked up the remote control and turned off the television and waited. Jodi sat and stared at the floor. He looked over at her and said in a soft voice, "I'm sorry it didn't work out. I just wanted you to start having some fun in your life. I've been taking up too much of your time. You're a young, pretty girl, and you should be out, having good time, not taking care of an old man whose life has already been lived. You should be meeting people of your own age."

"I know what you're doing." Jodi said, interrupting him, "I know men aren't all bad, like Lloyd and my dad. I am young and I'm in no hurry. I have plenty of time to find Mr. Right, and I will someday, but please don't rush me. I feel like you're trying to push me out and right now I need you even more than you need me. I'll be fine. I know there is a soul mate out there for me. But he'll just have to wait, and if he is real he will wait." She sat and looked up at the ceiling and took a deep breath and looked back at Quinn. She was so used to being pushed out, she felt like it was starting all over again.

"My place in life right now is with you. I know this to be the honest truth. I love being here. I've never known anyone who made me feel at peace with myself until you came into my life. Please, let me enjoy it a little longer." She stopped and looked off to the side then down at the floor again.

Quinn got up and walked over and sat next to her. He put his arm around her shoulder. "Oh, Jodi, I never meant to hurt you...I'm sorry. I'm just an insensitive old man trying to look out for what's best for you, and I guess I'm not doing a very good job of it."

"No you're not, and stop calling yourself an old man. You're not old at all. Did you ever look around that home you were in? Well that's old. You might be insensitive at times, but that's just a guy thing."

Quinn grinned and kissed her on the top of her head.

"So, what did you fix me for a homecoming dinner?" Jodi asked.

"Nothing. Here I go being insensitive again."

"That's okay, we'll fix something together, and no more of this heavy conversation, agreed?"

"It's your call." Quinn said, glad that was over with. He never was very good at deep, intimate conversations. They went into the kitchen together but he let Jodi do all the cooking, and eventually he worked his way back to his chair and sat down. He was tired. It was all that confusion and talking that made him weary. He sat and watched television until Jodi called him in for dinner. He had been having trouble sleeping and he wasn't very hungry, so he didn't eat much and went to bed early.

Quinn looked around and found himself in a dark, hazy fog. Someone was laughing off in the distance. Then the laughter drifted off as though it were being carried away by the wind. He strained his senses to locate where the laughter had come from, and then he heard it again, louder this time. He stopped to listen, trying to fix his sight upon it. He slowly made out a listless, wavering figure through the haze in front of him, beckoning him forward. It was holding something in its hand and held it out for Quinn to see.

"What do you want?"

"Come here, I want to show you something."

Quinn moved closer. "What do you want to show me?"

"Look, do you see it?"

Quinn rubbed his eyes and stared through the thick fog. "What is it?"

"It's a gun."

Quinn tried to focus his eyes on the gun, "What are you going to do with it?"

"I'm going to kill you"

Quinn backed off, then turned and began to run. He could hear the laughing again. He tripped over something and fell to the ground. It looked like a small, white dog. He jerked his head around and looked back and saw a bright flash of light, as a missile slowly came towards him. He moved to the side but it kept coming. Everywhere he moved it followed him. He heard a voice—it was Jodi's. "Look out, Jodi!"

"Quinn, Quinn it's all right, it's all right! It just a dream! You're dreaming."

He sat up abruptly, opening his eyes. Jodi was standing next to his bed. "It was Lloyd, he's come back."

"No, Quinn, it was just a dream, Lloyd's dead."

"No, he was here, I saw him."

"You were dreaming. I heard you from my room and when I came in you were thrashing around in the bed. It's all right now, it's all right."

"It was so real."

"I know, I have had dreams like that…about Lloyd…" She sat on his bed and held his hand.

"I've been having bad dreams lately, but nothing like this." Quinn was shaken and felt helpless, like a little child.

"It was Lloyd… I know it was." Quinn whispered, his voice trembling, "He came back. I could see the flash of his gun and the bullet coming at me moving real slow. I'd moved to the side and it just kept coming at me. I couldn't get away."

"It's all right now, lie down and try and relax. I'll stay here with you."

Quinn lay back down, and Jodi lay on the bed next to him holding his hand. She leaned over and kissed him softly on the cheek. "You're cold," Quinn said, "Here, put the covers over you."

Jodi slid under the covers next to him and put her arm on his chest and kissed him again on the cheek. Quinn at last began to calm himself. It felt comforting, less alone, having her there beside him. She warmed him and her breath smelled sweet. He began to relax and his breathing became normal and quiet.

"I've never in my life had so many bad dreams before. I'm going to toss those pills the doctor gave me."

Quinn turned his head towards her and their lips touched so slightly for a moment. Jodi gazed into his eyes. "I want to make love to you, Quinn."

There was long silent pause. Quinn's heart began to beat fast and he was getting nervous all over again. Here was this young, pretty girl lying next to him, offering herself. He felt temptation sweeping over him, his blood warming as it flowed through his veins. This was no dream.

"Did you hear me?" Jodi said softly in his ear.

Quinn put a finger up to her lips to hush her. "Go to sleep, Jodi. Go to sleep." They were quiet now, with just the sound of their breathing. They lay together in each other's arms and Quinn gave her hand a little squeeze, and they slept.

# CHAPTER SIXTEEN

Quinn heard Jodi get out of bed and go back to her room while he cowardly pretended he was still sleeping. He thought she was doing the right thing, but now he was having trouble going back to sleep. His mind was filled with guilt. There were feelings coming from every direction. How could he bring a young female friend into their bed? He thought maybe he had been unfaithful to Emma. Emma had always told him "You can't stop living; your life will go on, so don't let what we had end your life". That was fine and good, but it still bothered him. Had he led this young girl on? Did she think he wanted to make love to her? And what if he did? He certainly was aroused. There was no discounting that. But it would have been even more awkward if they were to wake up in the morning, in bed together. She must have known that, and he guessed that's why she left and went back to her room. She might have thought he'd think she was of low morals and just playing games with him. Or was he playing games with her. He wasn't sure.

He wondered if their close, almost romantic moment was going to change their relationship. Nothing really had happened. Had he wanted it to happen? What old man wouldn't want a pretty young girl to make love to him? It sure felt right, but he knew it would never end well. That's the thing about being old, you're aware of endings. Should he pretend that she never said anything? Will she remember the words she whispered to him? He knew that he always would. But was she trying to trap him into some kind of relationship? He knew that he was getting more and more independent, and soon he wouldn't need her at all. So what should he say to her? I'm fine now, just like new, so thank you very much, and have a good life. Then tell her to leave?

Finally, he found himself wondering how that warm, tender moment, as they lay in each other's arms, had become so terrible. Quinn fluffed up his pillow, rolled over onto his side and slowly went back to sleep. He knew that they both knew that this attraction, or whatever it was, would come to an end someday. Like everything in life, it too was in constant change. No matter how hard either of them thought about it, neither of them knew how it was going to change or end. They would just have to wait and see.

Quinn woke up and stretched out his arms and felt the bed next to him, then remembered that Jodi had left him sometime during the night. He hoped she wasn't upset about what happened, but he knew it must be bothering her. Jodi had always made an effort to do the right thing since she'd been there, and last night…Well now that it's morning, and as he looked back on it, he didn't think that there was anything wrong, but he had better go find her and knock the guilt off her shoulders.

He got dressed and went into the kitchen and started the coffee. There was no sign of Jodi anywhere in the house. Now he knew she was having trouble dealing with it. She was probably hiding outside in the barn. He'd have to be careful how he handled this and not say anything that would make it worse.

He opened the back door and stepped outside, taking in the clean, crisp morning air. He reached behind his back and took hold of his pants and hiked them up, then started down the steps towards the barn, glancing around as he went along. It was cool, and the sun shone brightly. It was going to be a beautiful, warm day, a day to celebrate; not the type of day you want to start off with a problem.

There was no sign of Jodi outside. When Quinn reached the open barn door, he stopped and leaned against the door jamb for a few minutes to watch her at work. Near the far end of the barn, she was cleaning the stalls and never looked up. He thought about what an honest, sweet girl she was and how hard she worked with never a complaint. Now all he wanted was to cheer her up and express his fondness for her. He finally spoke up in his warmest, most sincere voice, "You're sure up bright and early. I've been looking all over for you."

Jodi didn't stop her work or look up at him but answered sharply, "I had some things I had to do."

Quinn leaned on his cane and took a few steps forward. "Come on in, Jodi. I made some coffee and I'll fix us breakfast. That cleaning can wait."

Jodi straightened up and glanced in his direction, then stepped back and leaned her rake up against the wall. She followed him back to the house with her head down, feeling very uncomfortable. She stopped at the steps and turned around and sat

166

down to remove her work boots, setting them to the side. Quinn was holding the door open for her as if he were afraid she might slip away again and go hide. Jodi stood up, pulled her gloves off and dropped them on the steps next to her boots, then walked past him into the house.

Quinn poured them each a cup of coffee. He set Jodi's coffee on the table in front of her and watched as she stared at it, not saying a word, just waiting to see what was going to happen. Quinn began to speak searching for the right words, so as not to alarm her. "Are you acting like this because of last night?"

"Yes, I am. I'm scared to death. I don't know what's going to happen now."

"What do you want to happen?"

"I don't know… nothing…I don't know."

"Don't you worry about it, you came in to comfort me, and that's what you did. There were no more bad dreams, and I slept well having you there next to me, and I hope you did, too."

There was a pause, and it was quiet for a moment, then Jodi said, "Well, so did I, but I said some things that were out of line."

"No you didn't, you said what you felt at the time, and I had to fight the temptation, but we both know it wouldn't have worked out. I would have been cheating you and you would have been cheating me."

"I'm sorry."

"No need to be sorry, you just made an old cowboy feel like a young buck, there's nothing wrong with that."

Jodi's head snapped around and she eyed Quinn, "I wasn't doing it to make you feel like a young buck… I was doing it for me." She turned back and took hold of her coffee cup with both hands and stared into it.

It was quiet again, just the sound of the clock on the wall. Quinn got up and took his coffee over to the sink and looked out the kitchen window. Then with a sigh, he said, "I'm sorry, too. I didn't mean it to sound like that."

Jodi looked over at him. "It's okay."

"We have nothing to be sorry about, it was a moment in time and it doesn't have to affect our friendship. We don't have to make it complicated, if we don't want to," he said, in hopes of relieving any guilt either of them might be feeling.

"I don't want it to destroy our friendship." Jodi said.

167

"Okay, let's not let it, then." He smiled at her and said, "What do you say if we go have a riding lesson, and if you still want to worry, we can worry about that."

Jodi finally looked at him again. "Thank you, for something else to worry about."

He sat down next to her and held her hand. "Last night you came to console me during a bad dream, and you were tender, and it only shows how caring you are for others. You have nothing to be ashamed about."

Jodi looked like she was starting to feel better. Quinn thought, she's taking everything quite well.

"You could have just packed my bags and thrown me out."

"Yes, but you're still here," he said, hoping things were right back to normal. She just looked at him, apparently wondering how he had managed to do that, something Quinn was wondering as well.

After they had breakfast, Quinn walked Jodi out to the corral to get her acquainted with Bracket. Her butterflies from last night's close encounter were now obviously becoming the morning horseback-riding butterflies. Quinn had her quickly moving from one uncertain event to another, without time to separate the two. Being frightened is being frightened, no matter what the circumstances are. But as she stood there looking up at the large animal in front of her, her expression changed, as if everything from last night seemed insignificant in comparison. The look of guilt had passed replaced by one of incomprehensibility: how would she ever manage to climb up on back of this horse and control him?

"There's a lot to learn about horses," Quinn told her. "But the main thing we need to do is get you on and start you riding. I want you to get use to the movement and the different gaits. Everything else you can pick up as we go along."

"Gaits, what gaits?" Jodi asked.

"Good question." This might be a bigger job than he had first thought. "It's too soon to explain. Let's get him brushed and saddled first."

Quinn was told not to lift anything over ten pounds, and his saddle weighed almost fifty pounds. How was Jodi going to put the saddle up on Bracket? He was beginning to worry they might have a problem here.

He made Jodi brush him down and even pick up his feet and clean his hoofs. Jodi was a little apprehensive at first, but with Quinn's encouragement, she managed to get the job done. "You know, Jodi, you're going to have to do most of this by yourself. I'm still physically limited in what I can do to help you."

"I know that. So why don't we just wait till you can help?"

"No, it will be best this way."

"Now I know what your brother meant about the way you give lessons."

"You won't forget, doing it my way." He was making it real easy for her to forget about last night. She might not ever forget how to ready a horse for riding, but last night seemed to be rapidly slipping from her memory.

Quinn held the lead rope on the halter while Jodi placed the saddle pad on Bracket's back. He walked his horse over to the saddle rack so Jodi wouldn't have to carry the heavy saddle any farther than needed. Jodi struggled to push the saddle up over her head and onto Brackets back. On her first try, she knocked the saddle pad off onto the ground and had to start over. By now she was perspiring profusely and sending out negative vibes.

"Okay, I can see we're having a little trouble here." Quinn's voice echoed the uncertainty he was feeling, "I'll hold the pad on so you can push the saddle up on his back."

Jodi looked up at Quinn as she stood bent over, holding the saddle that was now on the ground in front of her. "A little trouble, you say? What makes you say a little trouble? How about lots of big trouble?" Jodi snapped back.

"No, you're going to be fine. We'll get it on this time."

"We, what do you mean, we?"

"I'll help you."

Between the two of them they finally got the saddle on Bracket's back. Quinn showed her how to tighten the cinch and shorten the stirrups. He had her put the bridle on and watched to make sure everything was adjusted correctly, then took a folding chair and went out into the corral and sat down by the stall door. Jodi took hold of the reins and led Bracket out into the open corral. It was just large enough to function as an arena.

"Okay, now put your hand on his nose and tell him who you are and how nice you're going to be to him."

"Really?"

"Yes, really, he wants to be sure you're not nervous or scared of him."

"But I am."

"Don't tell him that. He needs to know everything is okay."

Jodi did as she was told, trying to sound sincere and straightforward and confident, but she wasn't sure how well it was received. Jodi was always a little clumsy when it came to lying, even to a horse.

"That's good, now walk him over here and I'll hold him," Quinn said. "Put the reins in your left hand and grab hold of the saddle with both hands, one hand on the horn and one on the cantle or back of the seat. Now jump and pull yourself up until you can put your left foot in the stirrup, that's it, now straighten up and swing your leg over and you're on. First lesson's over."

Jodi turned in surprise. "That's it?"

"I'm just kidding. How do you feel?"

"I'm feeling fine, I'm feeling just fine. It's sure a long ways to the ground."

"Now loosen up on the reins and give him a little kick, not hard, just a nudge with your heels to get him walking. That's it, sit up straight and keep your butt in the seat and get a rhythm going with the horse. Let your body flow with the horse, stay centered and don't lean to one side or the other. That's good, just keep him walking around till he gets used to you and you to him. Do you feel more relaxed now?"

"Yes." Her voice sounded timid and unsure. He knew she was lying.

She sure wasn't any Emma. Emma got on a horse and became one with it. But it wasn't fair to compare the two. Emma had spent her whole life riding horses and Jodi had never done anything like this. In her whole life, Jodi had never had any outside activities. He was going to have to take it really slow with her. He didn't want to scare her or frighten her off.

"I know you feel nervous. You don't have to do this if you don't want to, okay?"

"No, I'm fine. I want to do this. I don't want to be un-American." And they both started to laugh. The laughing helped calm her nerves, and she felt more relaxed. She walked Bracket around the corral a few more times.

Quinn told her to lay the right rein against the side of his neck. "He'll turn around." And to Jodi's obvious amazement, he did. Then they started around in the other direction. "When you want to stop, just pull back on the reins a little and say, whoa." She rode around a few more times and turned him around and rode back the other direction. She kept it up for about fifteen minutes, then finally rode up to Quinn with a slight grin on her face, stopped and got off on her own. "I feel so stupid." Jodi said.

"Why? You did great. It's all going to take some time."

"But all I did was walk around in a circle."

"I know, we're just taking baby steps. Just like me. I can't even get on him yet. We'll work on it together.'

"I think I will like riding. I know I like your horse. He was very patient with me." Jodi walked Bracket into the barn and took his saddle off and carried it to the saddle rack. It was a lot easier taking the saddle off than putting it on. She brushed him and put him in his stall. "Next time we use Jesse's saddle, it's lighter than mine," Quinn said.

"It's lighter? Well, now is a good time to think of that." Jodi responded. "You know muscles are not my strongest attribute."

"I know, it's your understanding of others in their bad judgment."

Jodi laughed. "Well come on, Quinn—girl, girl's saddle. Does it have a ring to it?"

"Okay, okay, so I made a mistake. It's just that I've always put my saddle on Bracket."

"If you remember, I put your saddle on Bracket. Already, I can see that it's going to get a lot easier."

They walked back to the house, joking and laughing about her first day's lesson and what was to come next. The days that followed were spent on ground work and lunging the horse in a circle so Jodi could see the different gaits that she would be putting Bracket through when riding. The lighter saddle worked to perfection. Jodi had no trouble putting it on Bracket or taking it off. She also fit in the seat better and felt more secure. Her riding skills were improving daily and by the end of the week Jodi was completely relaxed and obviously feeling more and more confident. She was coming along a lot faster than Quinn was. He still could not stand for long intervals and gave the lessons mostly sitting in the folding chair. He was going to give himself another week before he tried to climb on Bracket and ride.

One morning he walked into the den and saw Jodi standing by the bookshelf, holding a picture of Emma in her hands. She turned to Quinn as he walked into the room and said, "She was beautiful."

"Yes, I know."

"Will you tell me about her?"

He swallowed and sighed. "There is so much to tell, I wouldn't know where to begin."

"Begin anywhere." Jodi said, like a small child who wanted to hear about a long lost relative that she had just discovered.

This was something Quinn didn't want to start. Quinn and Emma had a very private and special relationship that was never meant to be shared with anyone. How do you explain what they had? You would have to live it to understand it. They could read each other's minds. They knew what they each were thinking and what they were going to say before they said it. Their love was bound so tightly together there was no room for intruders. What could he say to Jodi? She would never understand. No one would. And no one had a right to enter their world.

Quinn stammered, then finally said, "Emma was a wonderful wife and mother. She did all the disciplining of our children. She would watch them walk their crooked mile, then reach out and catch them before they fell. She was a great lover and friend. Always full of fun and laughter, she could dance better than anyone. Emma had more friends than anyone I've ever known, and they all came to her at times for advice. It was as if they were all her children. Emma always made time for them. She had her moments and she could get her Irish up. But she loved everyone in her own way. She would have liked you, Jodi." Quinn got quiet now; he's said all the easy things and didn't feel like saying any more. He turned and walked into the kitchen and poured himself a cup of coffee and went outside.

The days now seemed to blend one into another. Jodi was enjoying her riding more and more, and Quinn was getting anxious to join in and started pushing himself to do more. He walked out to the barn one night alone and started cleaning his saddle. It was sitting on a saddle rack, and as he started wiping off the dust, he picked up one end of the saddle and then the other. It seemed so heavy. He didn't remember it being this heavy. He set it back down and picked it up again. He kept doing this over and over, like he was in a gym working out with weights. He was going to do it. He was going to start riding again. He might need Jodi's help getting the saddle on, and wouldn't that be something, he thought. She'd work that for whatever it was worth.

Quinn called his brother at the ranch and told him he needed another horse for a week or so. Will asked how he was feeling and about Jodi's riding lesson and Quinn told him she was coming along real fast and it all had to do with his teaching technique.

Will came back with a quick "bullshit."

And Quinn said, "No, really, she's picking things up really fast."

"Well, she must have some natural ability, then."

"So you're not going to give me any credit at all?"

"Nope, but I have an eight-year old mare, that's real trail smart," Will told Quinn. "The horse needs to be ridden, so you would be doing me a favor to work her for me."

"That sounds perfect."

"You keep her as long as you need her. I'll have one of my boys bring her over."

"Thanks, Will, I really appreciate it."

"So you're going to start riding again? You're not rushing it, are you? I would hate to see you undo all the healing you've been through, in one day on a horse."

"No, I promise, my body is ready for this. I'm going to take it slow and easy."

"I sure hope so. Don't you go showing off and do something stupid, okay?"

"Don't worry, I won't."

"Well, history tells me different."

"Look, I don't want to be in anymore pain. I've already been there. So I'm going to be real smart about this, believe me."

He was glad that Will was sending over another horse. He needed to start riding with Jodi and get her out of the confinement of his small arena and once he got her out on the trails and up into the hills, she could really start to experience the fun of riding and what it was all about.

They started out in the early morning, riding side by side, out his driveway and up the street to the bridle path. It was the same beginning as all of his rides. It felt right being on his horse again. Quinn decided to take Jodi on a nice, easy trail to start her out, just so she could get the feel of being out in the open without a fence around her. He'd take her up into the high hills so she could feel the freedom of an unenclosed environment where she could breathe the fresh air and look out over the world and shed the feelings of always being shut in.

This was the first time Quinn had ridden in almost six months. He felt a little stiff and what pain he felt was tolerable. The ride lasted about an hour, and by the time they got back to the house, they were both a little sore. Jodi seemed to enjoy being out in the open air and on the hillsides. She'd shown no signs of fear when riding up and down the steep trails.

They went riding almost daily. Sometimes they didn't start out until late in the afternoon, and by the time they returned it was after dark. Jodi was having the time of her life. But she knew with Quinn's constant improvement, her stay was coming to an end.

Jodi dreaded the day that she would have to leave. But it was time, time to go back to work, back to school and on with her life. She re-registered for the next term at school and called about getting her job back at the coffee shop. She was honestly surprised at how eager they were to have her back. "They even gave me a raise and promotion to cashier and hostess!" she excitedly told Quinn.

"Not surprised."

He could see that she felt a deep sadness about leaving him and her new-found way of life. They both knew that her school and new job would help her in the transition back to her old ways. But it was going to be hard, and it was obvious that she already felt the sadness creeping into her soul. Jodi told him that when she sat alone in her room at night, she thanked God for letting her spend this time in her life here at his home, and that the memories would stay with her forever.

"I thanked Him too, Jodi."

It was the middle of the afternoon on a Saturday. The sky was clear and the air was warm. Jodi had just given the horses a bath and was walking back to the house when Anna and Robert drove up in separate cars. By now they'd all become good friends, and Jodi was glad to see them. Quinn walked out of the house and down the steps to the driveway, and they stood around and talked for a few minutes.

Anna went up to Jodi and put her arms around her and gave her a hug. "Jodi, we have a gift for you. We know you won't take payment for all you've done for Dad. So you're going to have to accept the alternative. We all chipped in and purchased this car for you."

Jodi put her hands over her mouth and stood there, speechless.

"It's not brand-new but it's real clean with low mileage and it won't drink a lot of gas."

Quinn put his arm around Jodi's shoulder. "It's going to be like having a new-found freedom that you've never had before. Now you can come and go as often as you please. We're not pushing you away. You might say we're bringing you back. You'll always be welcome here, like a home away from home."

Jodi started crying. She couldn't stop crying. She was so happy and excited, she didn't know what to say.

"You can't say no," Anna said, "because the car is already registered in your name and insured for one year."

Jodi looked back and forth at each person, tears running down her face. "No, yes, yes, I love it. I love all of you, Thank you all so much. I don't know what to say, you make me feel like the happiest person in the world."

The happiness turned to sadness as Jodi packed up the few things she had and prepared to leave. Quinn walked her out to her new car. "Isn't it beautiful, Quinn? I just love it." They stood and held each other for a long time. They were both going to miss each other much more than they realized. She could always come back to visit whenever she wanted, but they both knew it would never be the same. That part of her life was over, it was already the past. Jodi's eyes were clear now, her tears gone, but he could see in her eyes that inside her heart was weeping. She waved goodbye as she drove away. It all seemed so final. Quinn watched as she drove out of sight then turned and walked back to the house.

It was evening now as he walked out onto the porch and sat in his chair. Sugar jumped up on his lap and stared at him. "Well, it's just the two of us now." He scratched her behind the ear. He had poured himself a glass of whiskey and lit up a cigar. He hadn't had a cigar or a drink in months. In some ways it was nice to have his solitude back. "You know, Sugar, I remember the last thing Emma said to me..." His voice trailed off as he took a sip from his glass and rolled the ash from his cigar into the ashtray. "Maybe it wasn't her last words, but I remember she was holding my hand and I was listening hard, for her voice was weak..." He drew on the cigar and let it fill his lungs before the smoke rose from his lips. "She said to me, 'don't ever lose your sense of humor or life will walk all over you.'" Quinn looked down at Sugar on his lap and patted her head. "What do you think?" Quinn looked out into yard at the trees, the spring growth just starting to break through in bright yellows and green. This was just about the time last year when he had called Anna and told her he was going to go open the cabin. "It's been quite a year, hasn't it, girl?" He scratched Sugar's ear again, "Let's get Bracket and go open the cabin tomorrow."

# EPILOGUE

Jodi visited Quinn every month for almost a year. Then it was every three months and then maybe twice a year, and finally just a card on his birthday.

Jodi had found her soul mate. He was a young paramedic she had met while working in Emergency at a local hospital. They were married and had three children, two girls and a boy, who she named Thomas Quinn. Quinn went to visit them once and was glad she had made a fine life for herself. They never saw each other again.

A few times over the years, Quinn would ride up to the high meadow where the creek starts because it was the last place he had heard her voice. Quinn died at age 89, and the family had a small service for him at the cabin he loved so much. They didn't take his ashes up the mountain. Instead, they put his in the creek that ran by the cabin. He needed a head start, they thought, because Emma's ashes had already passed by.

CPSIA information can be obtained at www.ICGtesting.com
Printed in the USA
LVOW01s0220070415

433549LV00027B/617/P